I0552659

Copyright 2021, by The Hilliard Institute
ISBN: 978-1-7342711-4-0

Editor/First Reader Teams
America: Lindsey Allred, Mark Hilliard, Rosemary Hilliard,
Kevin Jones, Jessa Sexton
Ireland: Siobhan Hoy, Amanda Kelly, Orla Kelly, Joan McDougall,
Noelle O'Connell
Cover Photo of Abbey Leix Estate: Emily Mae Bergeron
Short Story Competition Judge: Andrea Carter
Cover and Book Design: Lindsey Allred

All rights reserved. No part of this publication may be reproduced
or transmitted in any form or by any means without written
permission of the Publisher.

All characters in this publication are fictitious and any resemblance
to real persons, living or dead, is purely coincidental.

Published by:
Hilliard Press
A division of The Hilliard Institute for Educational Wellness

Franklin, Tennessee
Abbeyleix, Ireland
Oxford, England

www.hilliardinstitute.com

THE POWER OF WORDS FESTIVAL

'Unlocked'

An Anthology of Short Stories from Emerging Irish Writers

Table of Contents

The Daffodils and Christopher Columbus

Siobhan Flynn

Every time I saw her my heart twisted a little. Something fundamental inside me squeezed a bit tighter. I couldn't have explained it, that feeling, which was a vague mixture of unease, compassion, and underlying dread. When I moved into fifth class – under the tutelage of the notorious Sister Francis Xavier – she was there, having been held back from advancing to sixth class, owing to her lack of academic progress. Her name was Cissy Hartigan.

I had been aware of her previously, of course, but to be in close proximity to her was to experience a spike of anxiety, rooted not only in her thinness and her parchment-pale face, but in the fact that she had the appearance of a girl whittled down, pared away by a burden of unimaginable responsibilities.

In another life she might have been pretty, without the purplish half-moons beneath her almost lashless eyes, the stringy hanks of unkempt hair, the faded, ill-fitting clothes and dirty canvas shoes.

She might have had a chance to learn her lessons, and not have had to repeat, as she so frequently did, in her thin, whining voice, 'I dunno, Sister.'

And she might have been spared the wrath of Sister Francis Xavier, a nun whose personality was marked by the absence of any sense of humour, and a fondness for inflicting strict discipline by means of a three-foot-long bamboo cane.

We weren't friends – Cissy didn't appear to have friends. What she did have was a clatter of smaller siblings, each one a scrawnier, skinnier, scabbier version of the next, scattered throughout the more junior classes. Her lunchtimes were spent in the marshalling and management of these little ruffians: divvying up meagre lunches; re-plaiting bedraggled hair; blowing raw, runny noses; traipsing to and from toilets.

All that achieved, she would sit alone on the wooden bench, gazing gloomily ahead, with her hands folded in her lap. While the weather was still reasonably mild, I had noticed her once or twice nodding off, to be startled awake by the clanging of the bell, and I was upset by the fact that when roused in this rude manner, Cissy's hands flew immediately to her face, in a gesture that appeared disturbingly like self-defence. But what affected me more than anything, what I found almost unbearably pitiful, was the sight of her hands.

Because the flesh of her arms and legs was pasty pale, almost translucent, her hands didn't seem to belong to her at all. Dangling at the ends of her spindly, blue-veined wrists, they were big-boned and reddish in colour, the skin rough and cracked, the nails savagely bitten right down to the bloodied quicks. Numerous times every day, those nails flew to her mouth, enduring further mutilation.

How devastating it must have been for her to find herself condemned to repeat fifth class, faced with another year under the merciless regime of Sister Francis Xavier. There were many days when she didn't attend school – she was hopelessly behind in every subject and subsequently unable to avoid the inevitable punishment, inflicted upon her with alarming regularity.

Another teacher might have, through sleuth, or tact, or plain disinterest, left Cissy to muddle through the curriculum in her own haphazard way. Sister Francis, it appeared, for her own unwholesome reasons, was determined to expose Crissy's academic shortcomings, and use her as an example to the rest of us, even when it was clear that no amount of entreating, humiliating, or caning would yield any positive result.

Friday mornings were a time of particular tension, when we had what Sister Francis termed our 'Recitation Session,' where the two pieces of English poetry studied over the course of the week were recited aloud by a selected student, and subsequently discussed by the class. If it had the potential to be a lively, even enjoyable forum, this was rarely the case, since it afforded Sister Francis an ideal opportunity to expose and ridicule the weaker students. As happened with that much-loved classic 'The Daffodils' on the first Friday of November, a day which began like any other.

Cissy, on this occasion, faced the class and began, in a plaintive, sing-song voice, devoid of any expression, 'I wander lonely as a cloud . . . I wander lonely as a cloud . . . I wander . . . '

'Stop it, stop it, STOP IT!' commanded Sister Francis, impatiently rapping the desk with the tip of her cane.

Sighing heavily to demonstrate utter frustration, she cut a vindictive glance in Cissy's direction, then faced the class, as a smirk lifted the corners of her thin mouth.

'Now, girls, which of you is going to come up and recite our poem, the way it is supposed to be recited?'

A rhetorical question – the class rustled and shifted uneasily, restlessly awaiting her selection. I scrutinized the scored and ink-stained wood of my desk-top, my eyes cast downwards.

'Carol MacDonald!'

Heart plummeting, I rose heavily and took my place, as instructed, next to Cissy.

'Now, Carol, "The Daffodils." Off you go.'

With a practiced flick of her wrist, she bounced the cane lightly against the teacher's desk-top, jauntily tapping out the metre of the poem, a little intro to my recitation.

At the edge of my vision stood Cissy, slightly knock-kneed, arms hanging loosely, head bowed, slack as an abandoned puppet. I didn't dare look directly at her, as desperately, I began in a low, rapid voice, 'I wandered lonely as a cloud, that floats—'

'The TITLE – we always begin with the TITLE!' The cane rapped out a sharp warning.

'"The Daffodils" – by William Wordsworth. I wandered lonely as a cloud, that floats on high . . . ' I continued in the same indifferent, deadpan tone. Then I stopped, and stared blankly ahead.

A wild and impetuous idea hit me suddenly – I would refuse to say the poem! I would accept the fall-out that would follow, but I would not become the harbinger of Cissy's punishment. It was a preposterous plan, yet I knew I would carry it through, because I simply couldn't rattle off a piece of poetry, then stand by and watch those red, ravaged hands being offered up for a caning.

I was acutely aware of the frisson of disbelief rippling through my classmates. Several were staring at me; near the front my best friend, Fiona Finnegan, was frowning, open-mouthed.

' . . . that floats . . . on high . . . among . . . ' I continued, haltingly, before stopping again.

A tangible buzz now enlivened the room – everyone was watching: even Lilly Finn, who had a Spanish mother and who sat at the back of the class, drawing cartoon characters in the margins of her copy books, affecting constant boredom. They knew I knew the poem – I always learned my English poetry. It was for that reason that I had been hand-picked by Sister Francis, to demonstrate to Cissy the full extent of her own ignorance.

I couldn't see Sister Francis, who stood slightly behind my right shoulder, but I could sense her anger, a palpable, barely restrained presence, preparing to unleash itself upon me.

Gamely, I began the opening line again. Someone tittered nervously when I stalled once more.

'Silence!' roared the nun, furiously.

'I can't remember it, Sister,' I announced, flatly, 'My mind's gone blank, Sister.'

Thereupon Sr. Francis whipped around, her long, sallow face suffused with a flush of incredulous rage. Into the awe-struck silence of the room, she hissed her final warning to me,

'Stop this nonsense. At once!'

But I was incapable of stopping – I had advanced too far along the heady path of defiance to retrace my steps. I felt an intense surge of power, knowing that Sister Francis could not make me say those lines, and it obliterated all traces of rationality and common sense. Somewhere inside I must have known it would be a fleeting victory, but in those few euphoric moments, it seemed enough.

'But my mind has gone blank, Sister,' I repeated again.

I stood very erect and kept my eyes focused on a map taped to the back wall of the classroom upon which the voyages of Christopher Columbus were charted in dotted lines, and in those few brief, glorious seconds, my mind did feel as free and formless as the unchartered expanse of water navigated by that pioneering Italian. Outside the high sashed windows of the classroom, a rare November sky shone steeply, deeply blue, and I sailed away past the Canary Islands, Madeira, breasted the formidable expanse of the Atlantic Ocean, on towards the West Indies. Time stood still as the pale faces of my classmates, their expressions registering varying degrees of horror and disbelief, seemed to hover below, rather than directly in front of me. I was engulfed by a swooning giddiness and wondered if I was going to faint, something I had never done before.

My flight of fancy was short-lived.

'Turn around!' The nun's voice was tight with supressed fury.

I turned slowly, almost dreamily, to face her, and I caught a fleeting glimpse of Fiona, her hand clapped across her mouth.

'Hold out your hand!'

I extended my right hand.

'Face your palm to the floor!'

The statutory punishment for not knowing your lessons was two strikes of the cane on each palm: to address my insolence and downright defiance, a more effective chastisement would now be called for.

In the deathly hush of the classroom the cane rose and fell, rose and fell, six times. The pain was on a level above anything I had ever felt, or imagined. I fixed my eyes on the silver crucifix swinging hectically back and forth on the taut serge of the nun's sloping bosom; the image speckled with the red and black spots which danced before my eyes. I bit down hard on my lip, chanting, over and over, inside my head, 'Cuba, Haiti, Jamaica, Puerto Rico, and Trinidad: the Pinta, the Nina, and the Santa Maria.'

'Your other hand, now!'

Again the cane rose and fell six times, crashing onto the tender skin of my knuckles. My legs turned to jelly, my stomach clenched with nausea. In the corridor, the pealing of the lunch-time bell got steadily louder; nobody in the classroom moved, or made a sound.

'Get back to your desk!' ordered Sister Francis, slightly breathless from the exertion.

She turned, almost distractedly, towards Cissy, who still stood where she had been placed earlier.

'And you'd better have that whole poem off by heart next week, Cecelia

Hartigan. Now, get out of my SIGHT!'

'Yes'ster,' replied Cissy, meekly sidling into her seat.

The corridor filled with the hubbub of voices, and our class was summarily dismissed.

In the lunch yard they jostled around me in greater numbers than ever before, my classmates, firing questions and comments as I blinked away the shock and pain.

'What *happened* to you?'

'Are you *mad*?'

'I thought she was going to *kill* you!'

'I thought she was going to kill *all of us!*'

'Show us your hands!'

Sensing drama, children from other classes milled about the periphery of my little group, to be shooed away by the bossier girls. At the far side of the yard, the teacher on duty kept a nose out for trouble. Cissy alone showed no interest whatsoever in our small drama. From the corner of my eye I noticed her, slapping one of the little brothers for some misdemeanour, he retaliating by spitefully yanking a fist full of her hair.

All my earlier euphoria – if that's how it could be described – had drained away, as the unfiltered clarity of hindsight began to wash over me in cold, ever-expanding waves.

Today's incident, I realized, far from being over, had only just begun. In addition to the fact that I would have to spend a further seven, interminable months in fifth class, there was also the matter of what my father would say, when news of my brazen behaviour reached home, as it inevitably would. My hands were throbbing, red-hot balls of agony, and I was still only half-way through the school day.

Girls drifted away. Fiona stayed, with one or two others, encouraging me, without success, to eat my sandwich. We bathed my hands in the frigid water in the girl's cloakroom as the bell rang for the end of lunch break.

As we filed into class, Cissy, for the first time that day, looked directly at me and I met her stare, eye to eye. Had I hoped for some small acknowledgement, maybe a quick glance of shared commiseration, or a fleeting smile of solidarity? I wasn't sure what I expected. But what I saw in her face that day was something else altogether, something which reinforced what I was slowly beginning to realize had been a foolhardy error of judgement on my part.

Her eyes were surprisingly clear in her pinched little face, and she gave an almost imperceptible shake of her head as our glances met.

Fool, she might as well have said.

One beating more, or less, was of no consequence to Cissy, and she was no more likely to know the poem next week, or next month, than she was today. In spite of this, she would proceed through school, and beyond, making out whenever she could, accepting the consequences where she couldn't. I, on the other hand, had been dealt all the high cards in the survival stakes, and had deliberately chosen to carve for myself a path to persecution, paved with the wrath of the dreaded Sister Francis Xavier. I had changed nothing, yet for me, everything had changed.

Her look told me that, in her opinion, I was beyond stupid. But there was more to it than that. Something else had registered fleetingly on her face as she had turned away – sympathy. I didn't have a word for irony at the time, but its concept was abundantly clear.

Cissy pitied me.

She pitied *me*.

Fr. Tom

John Geoghegan

*A serpent deceived Eve into eating fruit from the forbidden tree.
She gave some to Adam.*

Fr. Tom walked into the Duck Inn as the evening light was fading. He looked forward to relaxing with his pint and decent-sized Jameson. The darkness of the pub shrouded him while his eyes adjusted. He walked slowly to a stool that fronted the bar, hanging his jacket from it. The TV on the wall above the spirits was showing horse racing.

'Nippy out there, Father.'

'Ay, Dessie, so it is. I'll have the usual, please.'

'No bother.'

He settled into his stool, cast an eye on the race, and listened in to a conversation somebody behind a pillar was having with Dessie.

'Did you see what won the last race?'

'No, Jimmy, what happened?'

'Backed him last week at Chepstow, I'd have been better off throwing my money down the drain. I think he came last. Now he wins there at a canter – I smell a rat, I tell you.'

'Ah, sure, that's horses for you.' Dessie didn't sound interested.

'By the way, Dessie my friend, have any cellotape back there?'

'Cellotape? I'll check in a minute.'

'Good on ya, you'd never guess what I did? Didn't I tear up the wrong flipping docket – I had a few bob on this yoke I ripped.'

Dessie handed Fr. Tom his drink as the mystery punter followed him from around the pillar. He stood beside the priest, surprised at first and unsure what to say. Fr. Tom saw him reflected in the mirror that sat under the television.

'Ah, Fr. Tom is it? How are you getting on? I hope they're all in good form beyond,' he pointed towards the church which dominated the skyline from the front window, its tall grey spire a beacon for miles around, a welcoming home artifice for the many migrants who had to leave the town as the recession hit in the last decade.

'Yes, Jimmy, they're all fine, thanks.'

'I don't see too many of your sort in here too often. To be honest with you, you're the only man of the cloth I ever saw with a pint.'

'I was just out for a walk.'

'A walk?' Jimmy warmed to the conversation, his open smile revealed a couple of missing teeth which through he hissed when he got excited. He held his pint in his hand and took a large mouthful as he contemplated his next contribution. He wiped the froth from his two-day stubble with his well-worn brown jacket sleeve and leaned towards the priest, one hand on the bar close to him.

'Still and all, it must be lonely up there in the big house listening all day to everyone on the radio and telly giving out about the church.'

Dessie returned with the cellotape and reached it over to him. He was an experienced barman and walked to a discreet distance, standing beside the dishwasher.

'Thanks, Dessie.' Jimmy put it in his pocket.

'It's great to know you can afford to have a few pints with your walk with collections down so much. I hear you'll soon be cutting back on masses altogether, things are sparse right enough. We'll soon be importing priests.' Jimmy looked to Dessie for approval, but Dessie was not interested.

Jimmy returned behind the pillar as Fr. Tom finished his whiskey. Dessie ambled to him. 'Jimmy talks a lot – pass no remarks on him.'

'I know he's harmless – he's part of the fabric of this town if you ask me. He must be a fine age by now. He hasn't aged since I first lay eyes on him.'

'How long are you stationed here, Father?'

'I first came here to Sliamh na Sioga twelve years ago. You won't believe this, but it was on my birthday, thirty-five that day.'

'I never knew that. I heard you spent some time in the hospital.'

'I did. I was Chaplin there for years. It was grand at first, but as the years went by I longed for more parish work, then this came up. I jumped to it. A small town, it reminded me of my youth, growing up on a farm on the outskirts of a town.'

Dessie continued to clean the bar, shining it in small circles with his cloth, his shirt straining to stay tucked into his trousers.

'Did you know the two curates who came before you? They didn't last long. One left the job altogether. I heard the other went to America.'

'No, but I was determined to lay my mark – I had great energy back then. You were too young to remember the trips abroad I organised, the youth club, parish council before they became trendy and so on. I took on as many roles as I could from births to deaths and all in-between. But like an annoying drip, it wore me out.'

Dessie stopped shining, put his elbows on the gleaming counter. 'Is that because of Fr. Andrew? My father doesn't have a lot of time for him, I'm afraid.'

'No point denying it, the whole parish knew he wouldn't lift a finger for any new initiatives I set up. We still don't see eye to eye on many things.'

'That can't be easy on you.'

'If it wasn't for the housekeeper, I couldn't have a civil conversation with anyone in the big house. The winters are the worst, just round the corner now, with the long evenings and rooms that never hold the heat. It's lonely up there, changed a lot since I came here, just like this town.'

'Yeah, I remember this place was buzzing only a few years back before the factories closed and the mart packed up.'

'Not too many young lads like you left. They sucked the energy from the town with the emigration.'

Jimmy came back from around the pillar, continuing his conversation with Fr. Tom. Dessie renewed his polishing.

'I prefer when ye used to wear them black clothes, soutanes and all that. We all knew then who was who. You'd spot a priest a mile away and probably cross the road at the same time.' He caught Dessie's eye.

'C'mon Jimmy, put that cellotape to use. I want to put it back where I got it.'

Fr. Tom raised his small glass. 'Could I have a refill please, Dessie? One cube of ice, also.'

Jimmy fumbled in his pocket and took out the cellotape. He took a torn docket from his other and held it to Fr. Tom as he walked around him. 'This,' he said, 'this will see me through till closing time if I stick it together. I'll have to hurry, the bookies close in ten minutes. Fair play to you, Father. The church would be a better place if there were more like you and got out with the people.'

As Dessie gave the priest his whiskey, he noticed Jimmy leaving with his docket held before his face for scrutiny.

'Here you are, Father. Fancy another pint?'

'Yes, Dessie, yes. That would be grand. Tell me, were you born here?'

'I was. My mother came from out the road. Dad moved here after they got married.'

'I suppose you heard about the curse, the píseog about the church building? Do you believe it?'

'Me, Father, no. But you know yourself things stick in people's heads for all sorts of reasons. To be honest with you it was so long ago I couldn't be bothered. I know what they say, that the church was built on a fairy fort site, but that was the 1840s. And the curse on the parish . . . I don't know.'

'Maybe you're right, Dessie. I'll tell you something between the two of us, I hate going back to that wretched house up there.'

'Surely things are not that bad.'

'They are, Dessie. Sometimes . . . ' Fr. Tom stared at his remaining whiskey. He twirled the glass, the liquid gurgled around the ice cube. He continued without raising his gaze. 'Himself, you know who, Fr. Andrew, comes down for meals, prayers, and to meet the odd person.' He looked to Dessie, 'I've the rest. To be honest, I don't mind at all. I like meeting people, but it's getting tougher on my own. It's lonely, Dessie, maybe that's why I sometimes lose myself in here.'

'I wouldn't say that, Father. People have a lot of respect for you. You did a fine job with the school extension.'

'Yeah, it's not that. It's just when I come in here I hope to meet up for a chat without having to do something the whole time.'

A number of people came into the bar, wandered to the back, nodding to both Dessie and Fr. Tom. Dessie took advantage and went to get their orders. One of them asked him to change channel as the racing was finished. He put on Sky News where it was reporting on a plague of locusts that was eating up anything green in Kenya, with food shortages predicted for the Autumn. It showed local people swatting helplessly as their crops were being eaten. Fr. Tom was listening to this when he felt a presence beside him. Jimmy had returned and was making himself comfortable in the seat alongside. He tapped his jacket pocket, 'Twenty-five euro, not bad at all.'

'Eh, no, Jimmy, not bad, a slice of good luck never goes astray.'

'I'll stand you a drink, Father.'

'You're okay, Jimmy. I'm grand.'

'You're empty,' he nodded at both glasses. 'Have one to share the good luck.'

'Alright, thanks.'

Jimmy caught Dessie's eye and nodded his order, pointing two fingers at Fr. Tom, his pint and whiskey to be replenished.

'Is Annie Mitchell still working for ye in the big house? I haven't seen her for a while.'

'She is indeed, still looking after us.'

'Some woman, how long is she there now?'

'I'm not sure to be honest, before my time anyway.'

'God, it must be forty years. You know we went to school together.'

'No, I didn't.' Dessie dropped the drinks, took Jimmy's money, and thanked him for the tip of the change.

'Ay, well for a few years,' said Jimmy. 'I left at 14, worked on the

O'Donnell farm for a couple of years before I got the job with Bord na Mona. Great people to work for.'

'You said you knew Annie years ago?' Fr. Tom had turned to face Jimmy, his elbow leaning on the counter. Dessie put coal on the fire that was smouldering behind them.

'I did. I know all about what happened.' Jimmy winked at Fr. Tom and looked about, conscious that nobody could overhear him.

'That was before my time,' Fr. Tom replied.

'So it was, but not before himself, your boss, Fr. Andrew, and others too.'

'I've heard stories, Jimmy. No point saying otherwise.'

Jimmy shrugged his shoulders and took a large drink. He was enjoying his company and warmed to his story. Fr. Tom finished his whiskey in one gulp and placed his pint in its place.

'Ay, Father, it caused ructions at the time, as much damage as those lads.' He pointed to the TV where a close up of a locust filled the screen. 'Does Annie ever talk about it?'

'No, not to me anyway, she's a private person.' He got down from the stool. 'Back in a minute, going to the loo.'

Jimmy sat back, warmed by the drink and his winnings. He felt the glow from the coal fire behind him as he saw his reflection in the mirror. He held his gaze and recalled the passion he held for Annie in his youth. She had hair like ripe barley, divilment in her giddy eyes, and as full a figure to keep him happy for years. He saw his life with her, an only daughter, a small farm on the bend by the river, and she having a steady job as the new priest's housekeeper. He held his glass remembering how it all had slipped from him. The scandal, the child, the hasty adoption, and if wasn't for the district nurse, nobody would know better. The whole parish knew the father was no stranger.

Fr. Tom sat back beside him.

'Yeah, Jimmy, a long time ago, as I said.' Fr. Tom finished half his pint, sighed, and pondered how much more Jimmy knew. He wanted to leave, but the alternative was not appealing. He looked up at the TV where was a new story about a racist tweet from a politician. He noticed Jimmy was almost finished with his drink. He caught Dessie's attention and pointed for a refill.

'One for the road, Jimmy? We might as well celebrate your good fortune.'

'Fair play to you, Father, I will.'

Fr. Tom put the money on the counter, under a beer mat.

'Ay, poor Annie was never the same. I was told the baby went to England. In fairness to Fr. Andrew he kept her on, her family never went short. It's a pity she never married.'

'What about yourself, Jimmy, never married either?'

'Ah, stop. No I didn't. I'm not saying I didn't have a go at it, tried to get my foot on the ladder, so to speak. It wasn't for me. I suppose. After a while you get used to your own company, don't you, Father? My ways, my contrariness, my own man, I'll only answer to myself. I'm a bit long in the tooth to change now. This is the hand I've been dealt, so I'll make the most of it. What's for you won't pass you by, is what I say. I suppose I was meant for me.'

Jimmy laughed at this, his mirth reflected in the mirror.

'Maybe you're right, Jimmy. Take things as they are. Listen, I must be off.'

He took his jacket from the back of the stool. 'Bye, Jimmy.'

Dessie was serving at the back. He shouted his farewells.

The farewell responses echoed in Fr. Tom's head as he climbed the hill to the priest's house. As he entered, he breathed deeply the aroma of shepherd's pie. Annie was tidying up in the kitchen. A newly-made cup of tea sat on the Aga.

'Ah, Father, your dinner is in the oven. I'm nearly finished for the day.'

'Thanks, Annie, it smells delicious.' He stood with both hands on the back of his chair by the table, fortified after Dessie's. 'By the way, are you in a hurry?'

'Not really, I've a cup of tea ready.'

'Would you mind sitting with me for a wee chat? There's something I would like to talk about.'

'Yeah, okay, I'll get your dinner first.'

He sat and Annie placed his dinner on the table, put a glass of milk beside the cutlery, and brought her tea.

'So, what's bothering you?'

'Nothing much, it's just,' he finished his mouthful of pie, took a drink of milk, put down his knife and fork, and looked directly at Annie.

'You know Jimmy Dunleavy?'

'I do indeed. He never shuts up, but harmless behind it all.'

'Well, I met him in Dessie's earlier, and he was talking about you.'

'I wouldn't pass too much remarks on Jimmy.'

'Anyway, he was talking a lot about a child, your child, Annie. I know, long before my time. I can't deny I haven't heard stories, but up to now we never spoke about it.'

'You're right, it was a long time ago, different times for all.'

Annie took a sip of tea, rested her elbows on the table, tidied loose hair behind her ears, and met Fr. Tom's gaze, directly across the kitchen table.

'I don't know how much longer I will be here, but over the years I've heard too many stories to concern me now. I suppose it's time you were put right.'

Tom had lost interest in his food. He wished for whiskey instead of the milk that was in front of him. This was not a confessional where he heard, forgave, and forgot about it immediately.

'I had a baby, a beautiful girl, Maria is her name.'

'Jimmy mentioned something.'

She ignored his interruption and lowered her voice, even-toned and confident.

'What they say is true. Fr. Andrew is the biological father. You see Tom, I loved him, still do. He did not take advantage of me. He was lonely, so was I. Two human beings fell in love. We weren't the first. I'm in touch with Maria, she was adopted. We got together a number of years ago, and we were reconciled. She forgave me fully. I won't go into the details of that. She is living in Scotland with her own family. Do you know I am the grandmother to two beautiful children?'

'No.'

'I am, so is he,' Annie nodded to upstairs. 'I know you two don't get on. I'll admit he is cranky and getting worse. Maybe the burden is getting too heavy for him. I will tell you one thing – I will never leave him.'

Any residue of Tom's visit to Dessie's had dissipated during Annie's talk. He looked around the kitchen, focusing on the red light beneath the picture of Christ before turning back. He could hear the wall clock ticking from the hallway.

'Thank you. I don't know what to say. Is there anything I can do?'

Annie sat up straight with a shadow of a smile, the only sign of the relief she felt as years of pent up anguish were released. She stood up, walked to the large Belfast sink where she poured her tea. She put the cup in the dishwasher, went to the door, and took down her coat.

'Yes, Tom, there is something you can do.'

'Anything, what?'

'Keep going to Dessie's. Don't run away like the others.'

In Full Pursuit

Jillian Godsil

This is a story set in a world where only one child is allowed per family; any other children are considered illegals and are hunted down and killed. The title is taken from Oscar Wilde's quote on fox hunting: 'The unspeakable in full pursuit of the uneatable.'

He pushed open the door and entered the warm room. The gas lights were dim and the fire smoked, but it was better than the storm outside. Peter shook his furs and stamped his feet; snow littered the ground around him. The barman looked up and gave him a neutral smile. Peter knew from experience that while he was never welcome, he was never turned away.

'What will you have?'

'A beer,' said Peter, looking around. 'Have you any food left?' It was late and the other patrons were talking into their drinks, a low rumble of chatter that clearly focused on his arrival.

'Stew,' said the barman, pouring a beer. Peter nodded, accepting the beer and downing half it in one gulp. It was thirsty work and lonely. Most other hunters that he knew were more than fond of their beer. Peter steered on the side of caution, on the side of angels, reserving beer for the night and eschewing spirits altogether. He had shared huts with hunters who rose to beer or spirits and it wasn't a pretty sight. It also made them uncertain stalkers; innocents were often caught in the cross hairs fuelled by a liquid breakfast. To be a hunter was to be a nomad and it was the loneliness that often led them to find solace in the bottle. Peter thanked his lucky stars for Maura, as he did often on a daily basis. Two kindred spirits – one ostracised for her healing, the other for his killing. Opposite sides of a single coin that spun through the air and had never yet found its landing place, its safe haven.

The stew was produced and Peter ate it hungrily without speaking. The barman polished a glass and watched him closely. Peter could sense he was curious and with good reason for Peter rarely travelled this far north. There was nothing or no one to hunt in these parts. When he finished, he burped loudly in compliment, pushed his bowl back, and indicated he wanted another beer. The barman filled his glass and removed the empty bowl.

'That did the trick,' the barman said. 'So, what brings you to our mountains?'

Peter could sense the interest across the bar; all ears were turned towards him. He could feel the curiosity quivering in the air. He burped again into silence and said: 'That was a fine stew, thank you.' Peter wondered if he should tell him or not. Sometimes he could get good intelligence from the locals. By the question, he presumed that he was the first hunter in the area, good if his instincts were right, bad if he was off course. He took another gulp of his beer. 'Illegal child,' he said. 'From the Runoffs.'

The barman's eyes narrowed. He spat onto the floor in disgust. 'Dirty, nasty things,' he said. 'We don't want them around here. No, we don't.'

Peter nodded. 'Any sightings then?'

'No, we'd have called the Constabulary if we'd suspected anything. From the Runoffs you say? They are a bad lot there. Always flaunting the rules. Just one will do, don't they get that message. Illegal children cause hardship always. Can't be trusted. They don't go to the Institution to be learned right,' and he paused to check Peter's reaction. Peter just nodded. 'Dirty, nasty things,' the barman repeated, polishing the glass vigorously.

Peter finished his beer. 'Is there a room free?' he asked.

'Just in the shed,' the barman replied. 'But, it's clean and there is fresh straw.'

Peter nodded. He was used to outside accommodation. His furs were old and hummed – strange smells of blood-iron, smoke from open fires, and sweat from chasing prey. A heady cocktail, it wasn't pleasant. When he moved to his shed, he knew the patrons would flap the air to try and get rid of his scent. They would not be so rude, or foolish, to do it while he was still there. Peter agreed a fee and paid the man. He would be long gone before anyone woke in this hamlet.

Morning came early, mists clinging to the side of the mountain, and the fresh tang of snow in the wind. It was bitterly cold and Peter wondered about his prey. Ten years of age, a female and no doubt scrawny. Illegal children were always thin and hard to stomach. The first one had been seven years ago, a young boy with burns on his face and legs where he had hidden in a chimney of all places, with a fire at the bottom. He had escaped, so maybe he wasn't that foolish, but it only gained him six more months of life. Peter wondered if the scars had had time to heal before he slit the boy's throat. All that pain for six months of life; Peter wondered if it had been worth it. The boy had taken a solid week to track and in the end it was tiredness, not lack of guile, that let him down. Peter dispatched him quickly, a mercy killing he called it, but the boy's face continued to haunt Peter's sleep. When tracking children the memories surfaced again and he preferred not to sleep, not to chance to dream.

Peter left the shed, which had been warm, and strode off in the still air. He moved noiselessly for a man so large. He was so far north he wondered about detouring to see Maura afterwards. It had been almost eight months since he had been here last, that time chasing a convict, a weaselly, skunk of a man. He had been sentenced to death for murder, an eye for an eye, but escaped before the gallows could claim him. It was Peter who found him and returned him to the platform. The City wanted to see convicts hanged but preferred to have children executed in the field. No one wanted to know about the illegal children, and even less to see them. It was an intermittent problem, usually flushed out by inspections, and areas like the Runoffs gave consistent trouble.

At the thought of Maura, Peter's mood brightened. When he visited she made him strip before he was allowed to enter her cabin. 'Leaving the blood outside,' she said. She would boil water and fill a bath for him. He stomped around outside waiting for her tiny kettles to boil enough water. When she opened the door, he would bellow and strip in a single gesture, before running into the house and climbing into the hot bath. Maura cleaned him with aromatic soaps and oils, anointing him for her pleasure. It was the one time his scent was submerged to hers. Sometimes she would join him in the bath, naked but for her amulet, an amber stone shaped like a cat's claw. She had been found with it as a baby – an illegal child, but found by a childless couple and so given a stay of execution. She attended the Institution with all the legal children, but she never fitted in. Now, as a healer, she lived a hermit-like existence. Without words, Peter knew he was the only man who visited her, but she never asked him to stay. It was just the way things were.

Peter walked on through the morning. Why had he come to this area? Some instinct told him the illegal had come this way. He had tracked her directly for some twenty miles before losing the scent. He had a choice – to continue on the seaward direction or move inland. He had chosen inland and upmountain. All he knew about the illegal was she was light on her feet and good at climbing. He looked seaward and at the mountains. A climber would choose the mountains he reasoned and so he turned uphill. This was his second day without any tracks. He was not worried. He had more furs and flesh on him, than she had on her skinny body. Either he or nature would have its way. He walked all day without hesitation; it was as if the wind carried an invisible code and he sniffed each time he stopped for new directions.

At dusk, he paused at the edge of a wooded area and looked around. Something caught his eye. It was a lone deer, grazing at the edge of the wood. He drew his bow carefully and took aim. The arrow pierced her eye and she fell quietly. Then he saw she had a fawn standing closer into the woods. He drew his bow again but the young animal slipped back into the shadow of the trees and was gone. Peter cursed. He would have liked to have brought both as a gift to Maura. Still, a deer was a mighty present and this was a plump creature. He swiftly gralloched the deer, tied up its hooves, and strung the body up in a hammock over a tree. He would collect it later and this way it should be safe from scavengers.

When night fell, Peter curled up in his furs and slept. He wondered if he was close to the illegal and if she had managed to find any food or shelter. No one in these parts would harbour her; the penalties were too high and illegals generally despised. 'Nasty, dirty things' the barman had called them and he was not alone. Peter's dreams were vivid again and he cursed when he woke. Then he stopped. He heard something: a tiny noise of a branch not snapping but being bent to its limit, a tiny creak.

Peter silently moved to the edge of the woods. He was hidden behind a tree when he saw her, pale and thin against the dark trees. She stepped gingerly along the wooded path, for there were many twigs capable of yielding their noises. She had no furs, as he suspected, but dirty rags of clothes.

He watched as she picked her way in the early morning light. She was actually moving in his direction. He must be upwind for surely she would have smelt him by now. He stood rigid as a statue hardly breathing. He didn't dare draw his bow for fear of giving his presence away. Slowly, inch by terrible inch, she moved closer to him. He could smell her in the wind, tangy and light. He waited until she was mere feet away from him before he unleashed his bellow and ran at her. The sudden noise and movement surprised her. She did not run. She blinked instead and in that moment, he had his hands around her neck. He was choking her and she made not a sound. Her eyes rounded and a single tear fell down her cheek. He closed his hands tighter and shook her frame as if she was a doll. Her hands rose then fell. At that instance, a chain fell forward from around the neck – a chain with a bright amber pendent. It was Peter's turn to blink, but he loosened his hands. He had been about to break the fragile neck, but the chain banged against his wrists. He removed one hand and looked at the pendent. It was of a cat's claw.

'Who are you?' he hissed angrily. Her face remained the same, impassive. Though her lips moved, no sound came out. Peter released her neck. He placed both hands on her shoulders and he could feel her body shaking. 'Who are you?' he repeated, but she gave no answer. For the first time in his life, Peter could feel an indecision rising in him like a volcano. He cursed again loudly. This death was worth more than 500 coins to him. He could live a year on that kind of money. The illegal looked at him. Her lips had stopped moving. Had she been trying to explain who she was, or to ask for mercy? It was obvious, even to an illegal or rather especially to an illegal, that he was a hunter and no quarter would be given.

Maura did not run the bath for Peter. He handed over the illegal and the deer, but not before cutting its throat and blooding the illegal's clothes with it. He watched the woman and the child stand in the doorway. As he watched, Maura closed the door and put on the bath instead for the child. Peter would not visit her again. He carried the illegal's life in his hands. Returning to the City he presented the torn and bloodied clothes and collected his payment. He did not visit the North again. He found solace instead in the contents of a bottle. His drunken dreams were filled with the images of the boy with burns on his legs and face, but he never remembered them when he woke. That was the one gift the bottle could give him.

Going Home

Mary Hanrahan

'Hurry up,' James shouted from the bottom of the stairs.

'I'll be down in a minute.' Anna took a last look in the mirror. Perfect, she thought, just perfect. She loved her new pinstriped bellbottoms, the flower-print shirt with the peaked collar, and she loved, loved, loved her blue suede platform shoes. They gave her those extra inches she'd always wanted and ensured that her precious flares barely skimmed the ground as she walked.

An old house was all very well, but these stairs were a death-trap. Maybe she should take off the shoes? No, she'd just take her time, one step at a time. She grinned to herself at the unintended pun.

'Ready?' Her brother was already at the door, key in the lock.

'You'll have to slow down,' she told him, 'Look.'

She extended her foot to show off the blue suede platform.

'Ridiculous.' He sounded just like their Dad. 'Where do you think you're going all dressed up? We're just going to Molly's.'

'It's Sunday. Everyone here dresses up on a Sunday.' That silenced him.

They swung into step, James shortening his stride to match hers. He was a whole year younger but already a good head and shoulders taller.

She didn't mind. It made her feel small and feminine like the heroines in Mum's Mills & Boons. Not that she ever admitted to reading them.

The sun was shining, she was wearing her favourite gear, and today Dad had finally agreed that James and herself needn't go visiting with them.

'They're teenagers, Phillip, they'll only be bored,' her mother had pointed out. 'They're going two miles down the road to Molly's. What harm can come to them? We can pick them up on the way back.'

There was no way they'd have been allowed off on their own like that back in Derby, but it was different in Rathduff, safer, her mum said.

Lots of things were different here in Ireland. Her dad was different, especially this year. It was as though he expanded with every intake of breath once they landed in Dun Laoghaire. He took up more space, his accent more pronounced, the vowels broader, flatter. He threw back his head and laughed more. He grabbed their mum around the waist, pinched her bum when he thought they weren't looking. He whispered things that made her blush, then he'd throw back his head and laugh again, louder than ever. He talked more too, expounding to the Uncles about his plans for the house and the adjoining acres. Maybe he'd purchase a few cattle, put in a vegetable garden. As for the house, he'd build on a new kitchen, put in a bathroom, and enlarge the windows throughout. Light would make all the difference.

The Uncles, always so called, listened and nodded and didn't say much. But she could tell they were pleased. Pleased that one of their own had bought the place, pleased that Philly was home again.

'It won't be long now 'til ye're home for good.'

Was she the only one who noticed the shadow on her mother's face, the way she smiled with her mouth, not her eyes?

She had overheard her mother talking to Aunt Molly as they prepped vegetables together at the large wooden table that dominated the farmhouse kitchen. Anna was curled up reading in the old armchair that flanked the Aga cooker. She knew the two women had forgotten about her.

'I won't let it happen,' her Mum said, in a curiously flat tone. 'I'm not coming back to start all over. The kids are bright – both Anna and James are going to Grammar school. They'll do A levels, go to university. The twins will get the same chance when their turn comes. That could never happen here in this country. Not for us.'

'You're right, of course.' Her sister-in-law nodded. 'He'd never manage . . .'

She said no more. The women shared a look, a world of understanding at which Anna could only guess. It was something to do with the reason they'd gone to England in the first place, something never mentioned in their house.

However, when other people were around, her mother simply smiled as Dad enthused loudly about the great deal he'd got, the fine place it would be when they'd done a few jobs.

'Cosmetic,' he said. 'Sure, it's as sound as a bell.'

Her mother never actually said very much at all, Anna noted, just nodded and agreed with all the well-wishers.

'Sure, it's great entirely.'

Coming home was a regular feature of their summer holidays as far back as she could remember. It was always the first two weeks in August, two weeks that were talked about and planned for from September to July every year. This year the holiday stretched to a month for the very first time because of buying the new house.

'Going home?' her best friend Sarah queried, her face puzzled. 'Isn't this your home here in England?'

'Oh, for Mum and Dad, Ireland will always be home,' she'd replied, but even as she tried to explain she found herself foundering.

'It's what we always say, going home, going home to Ireland.'

'It's great to have ye home,' that's what everyone else always said too, when they visited the various relations who all seemed to live within a ten mile radius of the village of Rathduff.

Every year, too, on the first day of the holiday, her dad gave them a pep talk about how important it was to behave properly, not to 'let themselves down.' Above all, they mustn't do anything to upset the Uncles. The Uncles were deferred to by all the family. There were all kinds of possible transgressions . . . being late for Mass, wearing too short skirts, being too full of yourself. It might be the nineteen seventies, but there'd be no 'notions' tolerated in Rathduff.

'Mind now or the Uncles will be mad.' Not mad, crazy – as she had first thought he meant – but mad, cross. The Uncles' displeasure was not to be incurred.

That was strange too because the Uncles – Peter, Davy, and Fergus – were quietly-spoken, easy-going men who never seemed to get too fussed about anything. Uncle Peter and Aunt Molly lived on the home farm where her dad grew up. It was Molly, energetic, capable Molly, who ruled the roost and kept her seven lively children in check. Davy and Fergus, two bachelors, lived together on an adjoining farm and took practically all their meals, except breakfast, in Peter's house. Molly sometimes joked that when she married one brother she got the other two as part of the bargain! Of course, they all knew each other's business and no decision, big or small, was ever taken without full consultation by all the Uncles.

This year, for the very first time, Anna had wondered what it would be like to go on a normal summer holiday, off to Bournemouth or Tenby like Sarah. She'd never even been to London and some of the girls in her year were going abroad to places like France and Majorca.

She tried to imagine two weeks of sand and sea, going to the beach every day with nothing to do, just be on holiday and enjoy yourself.

Not that she didn't love her aunts and uncles and all her cousins. They were 'great gas' as they said themselves and, to be fair, she had a lot more freedom over here. She and James could go walking or cycling with her cousins, calling into the creamery shop at the crossroads to buy chewy bars and red lemonade. They could take off across the fields with a picnic, go fishing for brickileens in the streams, stay out 'til supper time and no one minded or came looking for them. Even the twins were easier to manage now that they were going on six and happier to spend time with the younger cousins. Plus, Mum and Dad usually took them along when they went visiting. It would be great though, just once, to do something different.

Maybe it was because she was older now, but she'd begun to notice that things were changing, little things. People called them *English, the English visitors, the English cousins.* Sometimes she could hear herself speaking, her voice an octave higher, clearer, sharper, a different emphasis on the vowels contrasting with the soft, rounded speech of her cousins. Well, at least people could always understand her. They looked at the twins in blank amazement, not able to comprehend a single word they said. Anna and James were constantly called on to interpret. She didn't mind, the twins couldn't care less, but James hated it.

'Watch where you're walking,' James said sharply, jolting her back to the present. 'You nearly tripped me up. And we need to hurry. We told Molly we'd be there at two o'clock. If we're late . . . '

'I know, I know, the Uncles will be mad,' Anna laughed.

Just then they heard a vehicle coming along the road behind them and they automatically stepped onto the grass verge. A large black car drew up beside them, the engine ticking over. Anna recognised the old man leaning through the passenger window. It was Patsy Foley; he owned the next farm on from Uncle Peter's.

'Well, who have we here?' he slurred.

'Hello, we're James and Anna . . .'

'Hello,' the old man sniggered. 'Hello,' he mimicked shrilly.

James's smile faded. Anna looked at him uncertainly.

'English is it? Don't ye know this is no place for the likes of ye?' He was getting louder. 'English . . . over here . . .' His small, dark eyes glittered malevolently.

The driver of the car sat silently, his profile clean cut, looking straight ahead. He was young – nineteen or twenty, Anna guessed – with dark, straight hair, good looking.

'The Fenians will get ye . . . and good enough for ye . . .' The old man was spitting now, drool running down his chin.

What was he saying? What did he mean? She glanced at the men in the back seat. Three men, indistinguishable one from the other. Large, bearded, all three with unruly mops of dark curly hair. One of them said something crude. Anna was sure it was about her. They laughed loudly, the old man in the front joining in with an obscene gesture. The driver stared straight ahead, said nothing.

She shrank back behind James, clutching his arm, feeling the tension in his slight form.

How well they had stopped here. She looked up and down the narrow stretch of road bounded by high hedges, no houses to be seen, no one else around. The whole world had shrunk to these few hundred yards.

Anna swallowed. She could feel her heart thumping so loudly she was sure they could hear it too.

'Where . . . you coming from?' That horrible old man was still there, still jabbing his dirty, begrimed fist at them, every second or third word an obscenity.

'From Lacey's house,' James explained politely. 'We've just moved in . . . '

Why had she worn these stupid shoes? There was no way she could run in them, no hope of getting away. Her ankles ached from the effort of holding herself upright, her whole body rigid.

'No English there . . . don't be telling me stories . . . Jimmy Lacey's place indeed!'

James tried to say something, his voice shakier now, but the old man drowned him out in another barrage of expletives.

This couldn't be happening. It was all wrong. Everybody round here was always friendly, even people they didn't know saluted them. They were part of the O'Brien clan, they belonged. She looked at her brother; he was white-faced, tears threatening.

What could she do? She was the eldest; she should be taking care of him. She thought of Molly, straight-forward, no-nonsense Molly. There was no way she would put up with this carry on. Suddenly, Anna knew exactly what to do.

She stepped forward, bending down, so close she could smell the old man's alcohol-soaked breath, her voice strong and sure, echoing the cadence of Molly's speech.

'Patsy Foley, you know right well who we are. Philly Brien's children home from England. Aren't you in the house above often enough,' she gestured with her hand, 'and don't you know all the Uncles – Peter and Davy and Fergus? Wait 'til the Uncles hear . . . '

'For . . . ' the driver cursed, revved the engine into life. The car sped away, the old man still hanging out the window, the men in the back guffawing. 'The Fenians will get you.'

'Sure they'll be . . . ' Anna's voice trailed off.

Brother and sister stood stock still, listening. The noise of the car ebbed away.

Overhead, a crow cawed, its harsh note echoing.

They turned as one, facing back the way they had come.

Anna whispered, 'I want to go home.'

Early Riser

Laura-Blaise McDowell

Hello and welcome to this month's episode of Into the Night *podcast, where we examine mysterious disappearances in the United States and beyond. I am, as ever, your host, Lyle Abernathy, and this is our first episode of 2017. You might wanna buckle up friends, 'cause to kickstart the year, we've got a special episode for you concerning the 1997 disappearance of teenager Lorrie Wayne.*

Lorrie famously vanished from her home in the suburbs of San Diego, California, while her best friend, Rosa Schwartz, was sleeping. Rosa always claimed she didn't see or hear anything that night, and that she awoke to find Lorrie missing the following morning. In the years following Lorrie's disappearance, her mother Beverly did everything she could to keep her memory alive, gaining national attention for the case by pointing the finger at the son of a local cop and accusing the county police department of a coverup. However, nothing was ever proven, and Lorrie has remained unfound.

This week, we got the chance to speak with Rosa Schwartz, Lorrie's best friend, who was there the night she disappeared, and who, twenty years on, has hit headlines by coming out with a pretty surprising new version of events.

So folks, we're going to get started today by playing some audio from Rosa Schwartz's interview on The Megan Rae Show *in January 2007, the tenth anniversary of Lorrie's disappearance. In this clip, Rosa details her original version of events.*

I thought Lorrie was in the kitchen making coffee. She was the early riser. Often, on mornings when I'd slept over, I'd feel her weight lift from beside me, but she was always careful not to pull the blankets off me when she slipped out of bed. Sometimes I'd reach out and grab her t-shirt and pull her back in, you know, just joking around. And she'd fall back and lay there beside me for a while longer, and we'd chat about whatever we'd been chatting about the night before, you know? But when I woke that morning I hadn't felt her leave. The bed on her side was cool, and I remember – this sounds silly – but I remember thinking she must have drooled in the night because her pillow didn't look slept on, so you see I thought she must have picked it up and flipped it to hide any stain, and, you know, plumped and smoothed it out in doing so. Lorrie was a drooler, especially when she'd been drinking. It was her secret shame. She'd kill me for saying so, but it's true!

(Audience laughs.)

So I had it in mind to let her know I'd noticed, to make her squirm, you know, the way friends do. Lorrie's mom Beverly had been on a date the night before, and so Lorrie had invited me to run over to hers – we always said 'run,' because when we were little we'd literally run back and forth to each other's places, and so even when we got to be teenagers, we'd still say 'I'll run to you at seven,' or whenever. Anyway, she asked me over and said this friend of hers had got her some alcohol—

This friend, now he's widely known to be the son of a local police officer?

Yes, he was Lorrie's co-worker at *Jeremy's Diner* where she worked weekends. Anyhow, by about midnight, we'd gotten pretty woozy, and

I was ready for bed before Lorrie was. She kept trying to get me to go out dancing with her, and I kept saying, 'Lorrie, your mom is going to be home soon – she'll notice if we're gone!' Her mom always looked into Lorrie's room if she got home late. And—

Now Rosa, what do you mean by going dancing, exactly? Were you and Lorrie frequenting over-twenty-one's venues at sixteen years old?

Oh no, not really, but we'd try our luck anyways. *Going dancing* usually meant trying to talk our way into bars until we gave up and went home, honestly. But it still felt exciting because we were sixteen, you know? Anyway, I'd gotten pretty drunk and tired by about midnight, so I said I was going to bed, and she said fine and poured herself another drink. We'd been drinking screwdrivers, thinking we were terribly grown up. Lorrie didn't seem mad or anything – she just wanted to stay up a while, so I left her there on the couch, and went to bed.

And that was the last time you saw her?

Yes. So then the next—

Your last image of your best friend is her sitting alone on the couch in the dark?

Well, the lights were very much on, Megan.

(Scattered laughter from the audience.)

Anyway, the next morning, I got out of bed to close the window, I didn't remember opening it, but I must have done it before passing out. I realised I was hungover as soon as I tried to stand. I felt achy and groggy, but it looked like a nice morning outside. The cars on the street were red and blue, and they reminded me that I'd had a dream that night about a red and blue hot air balloon. And I thought, through my grogginess, that I must ask Lorrie her opinion on hot air balloons, because she had an opinion on everything. It would probably be the opposite of whatever I said *(laughs),* but I wanted to know what she thought anyway, and I wanted some coffee, and I could smell it brewing. So I got dressed and went out of the room.

The apartment Lorrie and her mom shared was real small, you know? The kitchen and living room were in the middle, and Lorrie's room, her mom's room, and the bathroom opened off from there. Mrs. Wayne was by the stove when I came out, and she looked surprised to see me. She said, 'Oh hello Rosa, I didn't know you were here.' And this surprised me, because surely Lorrie would have mentioned I'd stayed over. 'Hi, Mrs. Wayne,' I said. 'I hope it's okay I stayed. Didn't Lorrie tell you?' And she said that of course it was fine, but that Lorrie hadn't gotten up yet, and she kind of looked at me as if to say, of course you know that because you were just in the bed with her, and I had to say, 'Mrs. Wayne, Lorrie isn't in there.'

I've never forgotten her face, the way it fell, and she clutched the front of her robe and looked around as if Lorrie might suddenly appear, reading a magazine on the couch or leaning against the bathroom door frame. Then she walked past me and into Lorrie's room. She looked around helplessly, I guess hoping Lorrie was going to jump out from somewhere, and then she looked at me, and I couldn't speak. I opened my mouth to say something, but nothing came out. And she said, 'Where is she, Rosa?' I just shook my head.

How heartbreaking.

Yes, it was heartbreaking. Absolutely. Mrs. Wayne came back into the kitchen and shouted Lorrie's name. I can't really emphasise enough how small the apartment was, there was quite literally nowhere to hide, nowhere she could have been. But Mrs. Wayne still ran from room to room. Maybe it seems like an overreaction, I mean I guess Lorrie could have slipped out early to run to the store or for a walk, but I think she knew, had some motherly instinct. She said she hadn't looked into Lorrie's room when she got in the night before like she normally would and had just gone straight to bed. She kept saying, 'I didn't look in, I should have looked in, if I had looked in . . . '

She said the last time she saw Lorrie was that afternoon – Lorrie had come home from work without her key. She thought she'd left it at *Jeremy's*, so Mrs. Wayne had let her know where the spare key was, in case she needed it that night. And Mrs. Wayne checked the drawer then, but that key was still there. She had me go over and over what had happened the night before, and I had to tell her we'd been drinking because her panic was making me panic and so I felt I had to tell the truth. She wasn't mad, but she asked to see the bottle and I couldn't find it. I'd left it with Lorrie when she'd poured herself that last drink, and our glasses were still there on the coffee table with the orange juice. But the bottle wasn't anywhere. We never found it.

Mrs. Wayne called the cops not long after that. Almost half an hour later, two of them showed up. They asked me what happened, and who'd given us the alcohol. I told them who had and then felt so guilty I cried. It seems so silly now, but I cried and begged them not to arrest him, and they laughed. It made me feel so helpless. I felt like, sure you can laugh, it's not your friend, this isn't your problem, you know? But I realised later that they were laughing because he was a certain person's son. They knew him.

I remember Mrs. Wayne was so kind to me then. She held my hand while I talked to the officers even though she was in a state of total panic, too. My parents were called and they came over, so then there were six of us crammed into the Waynes' tiny apartment. Once I'd told the cops everything I could, my parents were told to take me home and not to worry, that Lorrie had probably just stepped out and would be back soon. I looked over my shoulder as my parents escorted me out the door, and made eye contact with Mrs. Wayne, and I think in that moment we both knew she wasn't coming back. I don't mean we'd given up or felt in any way resigned, but when I think of that look we shared, I can't help but feel that that was what was communicated, a knowing. Then one of the officers shifted his footing, and obscured Mrs. Wayne from me.

So you don't think Lorrie's ever coming home?

Well, it's not that, but I mean. She hasn't, you know? It's been ten years. It's not that I don't think there's a chance, it's not that I don't hope, but . . . in retrospect it feels like I knew right away we'd be waiting a long time.

Interesting. And tell us, Rosa, what happened then? What was life like for you immediately after your best friend disappeared forever?

Well, I . . . You see, I was as baffled and upset as everybody else, if not more so, because I felt embarrassed. Initially, everybody was saying she ran away, and that meant they all thought that my best friend had ditched me in the middle of the night. I felt made a fool of, honestly. Even though deep down I knew that wasn't what happened, that Lorrie wouldn't have done that. And Mrs. Wayne had seen I was telling the truth when we had made the discovery of Lorrie's disappearance together. But honestly, I think to this day she might be the only one who truly believes me. I had to tell and retell the events of that night so many times that they lost all meaning – you know like if you say a word over and over it just becomes sound, noise, that's what my story became. I started to feel crazy, to second guess myself with all the questions everybody asked me.

Everybody, as in, the police?

Ha! The police hardly asked me anything. It was everybody else doing the talking, friends, family, neighbours. Everyone wanted to know. 'How drunk was she? How drunk were you? Could you have had a fight and not remember? Did she seem mad you wouldn't go dancing? Was anyone else there? Did *that friend* come over with the alcohol? Did something happen with him? Could she have gone to meet him? Could he have come in the window? Could he have been there the whole time?' The police couldn't have had less interest in him.

Lorrie's mom, Beverly, who I understand you're still in touch with, has publicly accused the county police department of a cover-up, specifically covering up his involvement in what happened to Lorrie. Do you believe this person had something to do with Lorrie's disappearance?

No. I don't know. I didn't really know him, that was the thing. So there was very little I could actually say about him or what he could potentially have done, or have been likely to do, that wasn't just total speculation. He was Lorrie's friend. Sometimes they'd hang out and share a cigarette on their lunch break. She said he'd make her special burgers with extra pickles. It sounded like they were heading for a summer romance—

But he was older than Lorrie by a few years – in his twenties, as I understand it, and she was sixteen?

Yeah, we were sixteen. It didn't seem like such a big deal to us then, him being older, but now I'm on the other side . . . That said, nothing had actually happened between the two of them, at least not as far as I know. I said that yeah, maybe it was possible she went to meet him, maybe she had his phone number written down somewhere, this was obviously before cell phones or the internet, but Mrs. Wayne checked her phone records for that night and the phone hadn't been used at all. Mrs. Wayne said she came home about one a.m., which meant that whatever happened had to have happened in the hour of midnight, between my going to sleep, and her returning.

Fascinating. Tell us, had you ever met him?

A couple of times, in passing, when I'd meet Lorrie after work, but never for very long.

It was a small enough suburb, as you said. You must have seen him around after?

Yes, I'd see him. I have seen him. Nothing more than that. We never talked.

You never wanted to discuss with him what happened?

No.

Why?

He never seemed eager to talk to me, either.

Okay, so you're not certain he had anything to do with it, but you also don't think Lorrie ran away?

Correct. I do not believe she ran away.

But the police concluded pretty early on that Lorrie was a runaway. That must have been awful for you. Was it awful?

It was a massive mistake on their part. Sure, they took our statements, did a preliminary search of the apartment, talked to Mrs. Wayne, talked to me, but they didn't really go any further than that as far as I'm aware. Lorrie was a pretty sixteen-year-old who wanted to be an actress, a socialite, a bright young thing, so it was, I guess, conceivable that she might have fled our town. I mean that it was easy to believe, if you wanted to believe it.

Look, Lorrie was devastated to have missed the swingin' sixties and seventies, you know? Like she genuinely felt grief over it, that was the kind of person she was, the level she felt things on. That was how well she knew herself at that age. I didn't know myself at all. I knew I wanted to ride in a hot air balloon, that's for sure. That was about my most pressing desire at that stage.

But Lorrie knew herself. She had too much respect for her own life and what she wanted, to do something so messy and unnecessary as run away in the middle of the night without any of her things. She wouldn't have left without saying goodbye to me, and definitely not without saying goodbye to her mom. I mean, she wouldn't have gone anywhere without making a spectacle of it. She'd have wanted her picture taken as she boarded the bus to wherever it was, Hollywood, New York. There's no way she would have unceremoniously disappeared like that. So yes, it was frustrating. Very.

Do you feel guilty?

I try not to, because I was a child too, and whatever happened to Lorrie, I guess could have as easily happened to me – we were equally helpless. Often in the years after, I wished she'd taken me with her, wherever she went, just so I wouldn't have to deal with losing her alone. But Beverly – Mrs. Wayne – helped me. She's been a great support to me these past ten years, and I've tried to be the same for her. She never let me shoulder any blame, so I owe it to her to be strong.

How beautiful. But then, what do you think happened, Rosa? What happened that night ten years ago, if it wasn't any of the obvious possibilities?

I just don't know. I don't know, but you know what's funny? I had a dream the other night, and it was so real. Of course, it was just a dream, but I had a dream that Lorrie was abducted by aliens.

Aliens? My goodness!

(Audience laughs.)

I know, it's ridiculous. But I did, I dreamt of the lights of a UFO coming through Lorrie's window, and Lorrie walking across the room towards it. I saw the window flying open, light filling the room, the curtains billowing in the wind. I was paralysed in bed, not able to move or get to her. And then she was lifted up off the ground and through the window, out into space. And then I woke up.

Well, I guess that explains the open window!

(Audience laughs.)

You were just listening to Rosa Schwartz's 2007 appearance on The Megan Rae Show, *marking the tenth anniversary of the disappearance of Lorrie Wayne. But just this year, Rosa has dramatically revised her version of events, and now claims that she remembers exactly what happened on*

January 15th, 1997. We were lucky enough to get Rosa on the phone for a chat about what she now says occurred on that fateful night.

Rosa, thank you so much for agreeing to come on the show.

Not at all, I'm thankful to be here.

So, our audience will just have heard the version of events that you recounted on The Megan Rae Show *in 2007. Why don't you tell us what's changed since then?*

Sure. Wow, you know *Megan Rae* feels so long ago now, in some ways. So much has changed since then. Almost everything in fact. You know, when you have a realisation as big as the one I've had, it really resets you on a core level, everything you've believed or known up until that point is no longer your truth, and so you have to relearn your own life. It's quite an extraordinary, humbling experience to have a realisation, a rebirth, if you will.

That does sound extraordinary.

It is. So yes, everything has changed because I now know what truly happened that night, twenty years ago.

And that is?

Lorrie was taken, not by anyone we knew, not by the guy Lorrie's mom thought did it, but by a supernatural force.

A supernatural force?

Yes. I now know that Lorrie was taken – abducted – by extraterrestrials.

Can you explain a little further?

Sure. I know it sounds silly, crazy even. But you said you've played a little of my interview on *Megan Rae*. Well then towards the end of that you probably heard me explaining a dream I had, or what I thought was a dream, in which I watched Lorrie being taken out of the window by a beam of light. At the time I only brought it up in a lighthearted way, to brighten the mood. Those chat show hosts try so hard to get you to cry, and I didn't want to give her that, so I mentioned the dream as a kind of comic relief. But shortly after the episode aired, I was contacted by a woman who's a psychic in Cassadaga, Florida—

Cassadaga, as in the Psychic Capital of the World?

Right, they've got a spiritual community down there – I guess it's kind of famous. Anyway, I know it sounds silly, and everybody rolls their eyes about psychics, especially in relation to missing person cases, but understand that there have been plenty of instances in which they've been credible. Etta Smith helped solve the Melanie Uribe case in 1980. In 1973, Pascarella Downey predicted who would be caught for Penny Serra's murder and how, and that came true twenty-six years later. I mean, Elizabeth Lerner essentially told police where to find John List, and they went and found him! The list goes on and on. These things are not totally dismissible. Anyhow, I didn't know all that back then, I just thought, a psychic? Please!

I mean yeah, that's what most people would think!

Right, the normal reaction! So anyway, this lady phoned me, and explained that she'd been having visions all her life, and they'd frequently come true, but that she'd had to move to Cassadaga essentially to be among her people, because ultimately her visions had alienated her from her friends and family. She told me she didn't come clean about her gift very often to people outside of her community, and the few times she'd tried to go to the police about things she'd seen, she'd been laughed out of there, you know? Understandably, I thought.

But anyway, she went on to explain that she'd seen my interview on *Megan Rae* and felt compelled to contact me because around the time Lorrie vanished, she had had a vision which matched my description of my dream exactly, but that in her vision she could see out the window, to where a craft hovered in the sky. She said that even if I didn't believe her, or believe my own – what she called – memories, that maybe it would bring me some peace. I said sure, whatever, thanks a bunch, you know? I really didn't let her talk for very long or ask her for any details, and then I hung up and didn't hear from her again.

But then just last year, Lorrie's mom Beverly passed away, and the apartment that they'd lived in – she never moved out of it – got sold, and I started dreaming about Lorrie's disappearance again. Almost as if Beverly's passing prompted something within me, a reliving, if you will. Every night I started to have these vivid, vivid dreams, and I'd relive every detail just as it had been, and then it would get to about midnight, and I'd go to bed and Lorrie wouldn't and then suddenly I'd wake up to blue and red lights filling the room, the window wide open and the curtains billowing in the wind cast by whatever was out there. I'd see Lorrie walking towards the window in a trance, her eyes open, the bottle of vodka we'd been drinking in her hand. I'd be paralysed, totally unable to move, able to feel a force holding me in place, and I'd watch as, when she got to the window, she lifted up off the ground and through the window into the lights. Then everything would go dark, and I'd wake up. This was every night. I'd dream the exact same thing, sometimes clearer, sometimes fuzzier, but the details never changed, and the psychic knew them all.

You say you were pretty skeptical before, thinking 'sure, aliens,' as most of us would, so what suddenly makes you so sure this actually happened? That it wasn't just that: dreams?

Well, these dreams had been happening non-stop for two weeks. I'd wake up and feel like I'd just walked out of a cinema in the afternoon, you know that feeling of disorientation, walking out into daylight after being immersed in the dark and the action of a movie? So I was going crazy, I felt like I wasn't getting any sleep, and I thought if Beverly had still been alive that maybe I would have gone over there and asked to spend the night in Lorrie's room to see if that settled whatever was going on, but of course I couldn't do that. I knew that I had to get answers, or else I'd never sleep soundly again.

I'd taken down that psychic's number, you know, just in case, and so I dug it out and called her up and I said, you know, "It's Rosa Schwartz, we spoke some years ago," and she remembered me straight away, said she was glad I called. I explained to her about Beverly's death and what had been happening, and she told me that it was normal, that what I was experiencing was an unlocking of memory. While Beverly was still alive, I was never able to fully realise what happened that night. My subconscious couldn't handle it. But once the only other person involved was gone – because you see, Beverly and I had made the discovery of Lorrie's disappearance together that morning, and we'd always kept in touch, it felt very much like we were the ones most affected by it – but once she was gone, my other half in this, so to speak, my subconscious was able to fully embrace the memory of that night, and that's why it had come on so strong. If I had allowed myself to fully realise it before, I think it would have ended any relationship between myself and Beverly, because obviously it sounds crazy, and she'd think I was making it up. Not knowing was painful enough for her, but a story like that would have been cruel.

Right. So, is it a crazy story or is it the truth?

Ha! I have to laugh at you asking me that because, honestly, it's both. I'm well aware that to most people I sound loony, and I know what people are saying about me now that I've chosen to go public with what happened. But I'm hoping my honesty will give other people hope, and maybe prompt recollection in others that this might have happened to.

Not that I think you sound loony as you say, but I do have questions. Why would aliens take one random teenage girl from a Californian suburb, and leave the other one behind? What were their intentions, would you say?

I had a lot of questions too, because I was, as you say, skeptical. I didn't believe anything right away, but I knew that something was happening, and the psychic was the only person since it happened who had ever been able to come close to providing me with an explanation of any kind—

Pardon me for interrupting, but you remained close with Beverly Wayne who was famously convinced that the son of a local police officer had something to do with Lorrie's disappearance, and that theory is pretty popular among people who know anything about the case. Did that never come close to being an explanation for you?

It didn't because . . . I can't explain it. It just never rang true for me. If it had been him, I would have woken up. Sure I was drunk, but I was sixteen. I'd had a few vodkas and put myself to bed. I wasn't passed out under gallons of lager or anything. I would have woken up if someone had come in the window, or broken in the front door. I could have done something. I could have stopped it, or at least gone with her. But I know Lorrie hadn't made plans to meet him, that boy. She would have told me if she had. She didn't have his phone number, there were no cell phones. She didn't even have a house key with her—

She thought she lost her key that day, right? Could someone, say someone she worked with, have taken that key and let themselves in?

Well, no, no because they turned that key up when they searched the house.

The cops found the key?

Yes. They found her key on the floor of her room. Even if she'd left everything else behind her to go meet him, or go with him, she would have taken the key or the spare key that her mom had left her. So no, that theory just never felt right to me. I supported Beverly in her efforts to shine a light on the case, and keep focus on Lorrie, but honestly, deep down, I never thought it was him. I didn't know what had happened, but I knew it wasn't that. I could have stopped that. I was there, and if that happened, I would have stopped it.

So then, when I spoke to the psychic, what she told me allowed me to make sense of what had happened in a way that I couldn't before. Also, these dreams I started having after Beverly died were a lot more vivid and detailed than the one I'd had shortly before *The Megan Rae Show,* and the psychic knew all the details without me telling her. Blue and red lights, the vodka bottle in Lorrie's hand, the fact that the force holding me down in the bed had left bruises which I found the next day, bruises on my legs, my arms, aching in my shoulders. She knew. It was as if she'd been there. And so I asked her, I said, 'You think this is real, that Lorrie really could have been taken by *aliens?*' And she said yes.

So I started to read up on all of this, and what I found was interesting. The general idea is that aliens take human specimens for studying, like we might collect specimens from a field, insects in a jar. They like to take samples from all over the world, all kinds of people, all walks of life. I think it was coincidence that Beverly was out that night. I think if she'd been there she would have slept right through the whole thing. People often say, you know, well, if aliens really do come to Earth, how come they only ever visit America? But people vanish without a trace every year from everywhere on Earth, in circumstances just as strange as Lorrie's, whether from California or Iceland or Sudan or New Zealand. And the craft, the craft that the psychic saw in her vision, it doesn't sound like – I mean, it's not a flying saucer. Her description, it's *entirely unpredisposed,* meaning it isn't based on the images we're used to seeing of alien crafts. It couldn't have been inspired by anything she'd seen on TV. It's different.

What was her description of the craft?

Well, it was like nothing I'd ever heard. Sort of a diamond-shape, she said, with red and blue light shining from it almost like a disco ball, opalescent, a texture she hadn't seen before, almost as if it wasn't solid, or was formed from a matter we don't have here on Earth, neither a liquid nor a gas nor a solid. Its edges weren't clear – I mean it wasn't clear where the craft ended and the air around it began. She said it was strange because it felt almost like she wasn't seeing it in the way she normally sees things in her visions which is as clear as if she was looking right at them. It was almost as if she was sensing it. She could see it, but she said sight wasn't the main sense used to perceive it. She said she felt like another sense, something like a sixth sense had awoken within her, and it was with that sense that she was perceiving the craft. Does that make sense?

Wow, that's quite a description, I'm ... I mean, I'm quite blown away by that description.

As was I, when I first heard it. She describes it so much better than me, but that's my own attempt at explaining it! I couldn't believe it when she said that to me.

Yeah. Yes. It's amazing.

But anyway, back to your question. I also discovered that often when a craft is doing an abduction in a populated place, a strange sleepiness will fall over those in the area, a sort of trance that means they don't register the presence of the craft—

But that didn't happen to you, though. You were watching the whole thing take place?

Right, it didn't happen to me, I guess, because I was in the same room as Lorrie. I could see what was happening, but that said, I never looked out the window – I never saw the craft. I think they must have done something to put me straight back to sleep or else I must've passed out, because I have no memory after that until I woke up the next morning. But, yeah, I know it's a funny one. There are a lot of questions that I still have too. Like why they took Lorrie and not me, as you said. Well, my guess is that they only needed one. I believe them to be scientists, unwilling to be greedy or overplough the land so to speak. They weren't going to take more than they needed that night, so they only took one, and I guess they took the best one.

Oh, well I'm sure ... I mean—

Oh don't worry, it hasn't hurt my feelings.

Haha, I guess we can't take these things personally.

Right. And Lorrie was taller than me, bigger all round, you know? She would have given them more to learn from.

I see. And Rosa, how have your family dealt with this realisation you've had? Have they come with you on this journey?

Well, not exactly. Honestly, I haven't been very close with my family for a long time. We all live in different parts of the country and – well, I mean, you know. None of this has ever been easy for them. Everybody has dealt with it in their own ways. I think they feel I should have moved on by now, you know instead of getting back into it? I think they see this as a regression, but honestly it's such a step forward for me. Such a release. The relief of this new life, it's almost like a new world.

Well, I'm glad to hear that. Tell me, Rosa, do you ever think you'll see Lorrie again?

Well, Lyle, I see Lorrie every day. I've started seeing her every day, now that I know where she is, all I have to do is look up. But yes, I do think I'll see her again, somehow, maybe when the light falls in my final days, my final hours, I'll look up and I'll see her and then I'll run to her like no time's been gone at all, and I'll tell her, 'Lorrie, I've missed you. I've really missed you.'

Rosa, that's about all we have time for. But it's been eye-opening and fascinating having you on the show today. Thank you so much for telling us your story. I'm so glad you've found peace with what happened.

You're welcome, Lyle, it's been a pleasure. Thanks for having me. And to anyone who wants to find out more about my journey, I'm online at rosas-journey.com and all my social media accounts link from there.

Thanks so much, Rosa. I'll be sure to leave the links in the show notes.

Thank you for listening to this episode of Into the Night *podcast, with me, your host Lyle Abernathy. You've been listening to Rosa Schwartz, whose best friend, Lorrie Wayne, disappeared on January 15th 1997, when she was sixteen years old. If you have any information regarding the disappearance of Lorrie Wayne, please contact the relevant authorities. Thanks again to Rosa for agreeing to come on the show, and thanks to you for listening.*

We'll be back this time next month with a brand new episode of Into the Night *podcast, so be sure to tune in, and, as always, stay safe out there.*

Final Curtain

Helen O'Leary

Morning. Another one. Lemony light filters through thin net curtains making new dreams impossible now. When sleep doesn't come, dark thoughts do.

Some days, she manages to block them. This morning already she's danced the entire second act of *Giselle* in her head. Every pirouette, jete, and arabesque perfectly executed before the clanging of the breakfast trolley breaks through her reverie. Brigid's low solid frame fills the doorway.

'Mornin' Miss Jane,' she says, dragging the trolley across the lino-ed floor.

'Aye, aye, Miss Jane, it's no wonder you can't sleep with the sun streaming through those nets. I'll pull the heavy drapes for you tonight and you'll sleep like a baby. Right as rain you'll be. Back to yourself in no time,' she says, plumping up the pillows.

Hefty arms pull Jane into a half-sitting position and gossamer dreams of light and curtains fade. But not before one final glimpse. The corps de ballet swirling behind her, white gauze skirts shimmering blue under stage lights, the audience on its feet, the applause deafening, her own sinewy arms laden with heavily-scented flowers. It was, they said, her finest hour. The entire city at her feet.

Sleep impossible back in those days too, mind spinning for hours.

'It's all talk of the Eurovision today, Miss Jane,' Brigid says, pouring pale, tepid tea into a thick, white cup. 'Don't suppose you toddled down to have a look at it.'

Jane rewards her with a snort. Agreeing to come in here was one thing, but mingling with the residents in the day room, the very idea preposterous! A step way too far. Waiting in the wings the lot of them – Blessed Oliver communing with his angels and that odious little Mickey McCarthy commandeering the television set all day, every day, as if life were about sport and nothing else. The rest in various degrees of befuddlement slumping lower and lower into their upright hospital chairs.

No. Jane had lived for the Arts. That's what her life had been about, and while she had her faculties, that's what her life would continue to be about. She passed the long days with her sepia-toned photographs, her yellowing newspaper cuttings, her programmes, and her faded dreams. Practice, of course, was still a must, twice daily forays into the long corridor, stiffening limbs freeing by degrees as she moved, the dado rail a barre beneath her arthritic fingers.

'I thought to meself watching it last night that it would just be your thing,' Brigid says, attempting to tuck a napkin under Jane's chin.

'What would be my thing, as you call it, Brigid?' she says, batting away the bib.

'The Riverdance. That Flatley fella with his bare chest, leapin' and hoppin' like his feet were on fire and all them young ones in mini skirts trottin' and tappin' around him. The crowd were on their feet a full five minutes, even our great President, Mary Robinson herself. Never seen the likes of it in all me born days,' she says, stirring two unasked for sugars into the tea.

Experience has told Jane that objections to the sugar would only lead to Brigid wittering on about meat on her bones and other such nonsense.

'Still, it was something. The roar. Put me in mind of Croke Park on all-Ireland final day,' she says, manoeuvring the trolley out of the room.

The morning papers are full of it. How they'd reinvented Irish dance. Talk of full stage shows, tours, Broadway beckoning. She devours it all with rising bile. That world, she thought, had beckoned for her too. Once.

Every caller she has that week – that whipper-snapper Doctor Sullivan (not a patch on his father, a life-long patron of the Opera House), the damned priest with his whiskey breath, and that infernal woman who imagines she is a close friend – prattle on about it. Hoping, she supposes, to rouse her spirits and engage her in some sort of chat. Ignoramuses, the lot of them! What do they know about great art, music, drama, or the beauty of the dance? All their pathetic attempts rouse is a sour lemon bitterness in her veins.

'Aye, aye, your poor feet, Miss Jane. We'll have to get young Doctor Sullivan to take a look the next day he's in,' Brigid says, heaving herself down on one knee. 'I don't like the look of that big toe.'

Brigid, like Jane, knows the value of a good soaking for aching feet, so although it's against Nursing Home policy, she brings a basin of warm soapy water from the kitchen on a Tuesday, while the manager is at the accounts.

'A few drops of baby oil, Miss Jane, that'll soften out those aul corns.'

'I'll manage perfectly well by myself, Brigid,' Jane says, 'there's no need for you to keep hovering over me like I'm an imbecile. I've tended many a corn and blister in my day. Blisters, Brigid, are the bane of a dancer's life.'

With fumbling fingers Jane closes the Velcro straps on her red velveteen slippers, a gift from the long-retired artistic director of the Company when he called last Christmas, or was it the Christmas before? Shoes, of any type, impossible now. Bunions like billiard balls, the price for a few short glittering seasons.

The ritual comes back to her. The bending and breaking of new pointe shoes, to make them more pliable. The sewing of rows of tiny white stitches on the hard toes for extra grip. The unfurling of the pink satin ribbons. Finally, the fixing of the ribbons, right over left, twice round her ankle, neat little bows, ends tucked in and a silent prayer to her god, the god of the dance, for luck.

'Pointless,' she mutters, lifting her leg from the water, 'all of it pointless.' Her life's dream had been blown to ribbons with just one fall, one bad break, and one badly-set ankle.

'Come on now, Miss Jane, don't be loosin' heart,' Brigid says, 'up you get, keep the aul circulation going. On you go with your practice.'

When Brigid leaves, Jane stands at the mahogany dressing table and attempts a porte de bras. First and second position she can manage, but third defeats her, her bat-winged right arm stalling at shoulder height. Arms that once fluttered like butterfly wings fall to her sides, useless. The face in the mirror horrifies her. Thin tendrils of colourless hair escape from her bun. Time was when ten hair pins and a filigree net could barely hold it, Brigid now managing to do it with three. Net surplus to requirements.

A memory comes, not of the stage this time, but of a drafty, country hall, the local solicitor's wife banging out music on a tinny piano. Her glorious career over, her life had been reduced to tortuous trips the length and breadth of the country in an overheated Volkswagen Beetle, drumming steps into clods of girls. She sees them now, rows of them, purple-kneed in short white tunics, trembling in front of her. Buns, hairbands (blue, pink, or yellow according to grade), clips, and nets to be presented for inspection. Such details mattered then. A stray hair could lead to a savaging. She neither got nor expected love from those girls, but respect, she thought, was a given.

'Lift those heads girls, chins up, and for goodness sake don't let those arms droop.' How often had she repeated those words, endeavouring to raise them to be something other than they were.

Once, some years later, in the foyer of the Abbey Theatre, a slender young woman had approached her. Apparently, she'd been a pupil, and in truth something in the woman's poise and gait suggested that. The turn of the ankle, the slight upward tilt of the head. It was the opening night of *The Playboy*. Back then she still thought of herself as somebody, and this woman was, well, nobody. Still able to command an audience, she, Jane, was holding forth to the who's who of the Arts world on the possibilities of fusing ballet and Irish dance. Turning towards her and bestowing a tight smile, she gave the woman little time as she gushed out her embarrassed thanks for teaching her an appreciation of the beauty of the dance.

But later, in the quiet of the night, it meant something.

Only to Brigid, months later, feeling that the end is near, does she bend a little, bare a piece of her soul.

'Did you ever want to be somebody, Brigid?' she says, clutching a yellow, plastic sippy cup between trembling hands.

'Be somebody?' Brigid gapes.

'Yes, Brigid,' irritation strengthening the voice. 'I mean did you ever have a dream?'

'Aye no, Miss Jane. Dreaming, where would that get you? "Don't be tormenting yourself with dreams, Biddy girl, and you'll never be disappointed," me mother used to say.'

Brigid pauses for a moment at the bay window, before turning again to the business of fixing the curtains neatly into the tie-backs.

'"Take that head out of the clouds and be thankful to the Good Lord for your lot," was another one of hers. But, do you know, Miss Jane, there was something in them aul sayings of hers. Making the best of it, that's been my way of keeping going.'

Brigid, it seemed to Jane then, had learnt one of life's great lessons in her youth.

'I lived in the clouds,' she whispers more to herself than to Brigid. 'Dreams and clouds. I always thought I'd be someone.'

'Oh, but you were, Miss Jane,' Brigid stammers, her kind, brown eyes filling with tears.

'Aye, I can see you there, centre stage with that flamin' red head of yours. Sure, that Flatley fella is only a child trotting after you.'

'How did you know I had red hair, Brigid?' she whispers.

'I looked you up, Miss Jane. 'Course I did. The name was familiar, knew I'd heard it somewhere. Took meself off to the library one Saturday and done me research. Said nothing to nobody. Sure, at home they'd think I was daft spending a Saturday in the library instead of catching up on me washing. I searched all the old newspapers cuttings till I found you.

'Oh, Miss Jane,' she pauses wiping a tear with the back of her sleeve, 'you were a beauty. A great beauty and every inch of you a dancer.'

'Newspaper articles?' she asks, 'Did they mention *Giselle*?'

'Your finest hour, Ms. Jane. I read every word about it and only wished I could have been there to see you in all your glory. Do you know the whole afternoon was gone with me imagining meself propped up in the Opera House and you making your curtsey and smiling straight down at me? The washing was all spun out by the time I got back and not one of them had lifted their arses from the TV to see to it.'

'Have you ever been to the Opera House, Brigid?' she asks.

'Ah no, Miss Jane, but I'm thinking I might take meself down there some Saturday, get meself a cheap seat up in the gods, and remind meself how privileged I am now to have a great star of the Opera House in my care.'

'Privileged, Brigid?'

'Sure, everybody knew you were somebody the minute you made your entrance here, Miss Jane, and wasn't I the lucky one, they put you on my list. I'm thinkin' that makes me somebody too.'

Afterwards, as the lights dim, it is a source of some consolation to her.

Somebody has noticed that she, Jane, was somebody once, and somebody is somebody for knowing her.

A Love Supreme

Patrick Olwill

'Sofia . . . Sofia . . . Sofia . . . ' It drifted down the winding street, an ancient plaintive chant. Over and over, the same three notes, pleading, longing, lamenting.

I closed the balcony window. Sofia still possessed me, images, smells, tastes. I needed to sleep, to empty myself of her. I lay on the bed, the air heavy and suffocating, but I could still hear him, 'Sofia.' I had to make him stop, but Ali wasn't someone that would listen easily.

Ali was a local beggar, half mad, often drunk. Back home he would be called a 'character' by some and avoided by people like me. Ali wasn't his real name, they called him that because of the shadow-boxing. He was surprisingly quick and nimble when he ducked and jabbed at some invisible opponent. The local kids tried to goad him into it, but he rarely did so for entertainment. It was as if he couldn't control it, like a seizure that came and went and had no reason.

Leaving behind my lonely room, I slowly climbed the narrow winding street. He was sitting on the crumbling steps opposite Sophia's building. He looked dirtier than usual, his flip flops next to the bottle beside his bloodied feet. I stood over him saying his name while he called hers. He pushed his dark matted hair away from his eyes and stared at me, focusing. He started shouting, words and sounds that were difficult to understand. I caught some Spanish but mixed with another language, maybe Algerian. Sofia had said something about him being from North Africa. I understood the tone though, he was really angry and trying to calm him was useless. His voice got louder, the words spitting venomously up at me until I had to walk away. He rose and followed me, throwing a flip flop at my back.

An elderly couple were staring now as I quickly rounded the corner. I hurried past the evening strollers, down through the Alameda towards the port. I ducked into one of my locals. Normally I'd have sat outside, but I didn't want to risk another row with Ali.

I ordered a plate of Pulpo and a bottle of the house wine. I didn't understand his anger. Why me and why now? I remembered Sofia saying in that vaguely enigmatic way of hers, 'Ali knows things.' Now I wondered what she'd meant.

I called Arantxa. It went to voicemail again as it had for the last two days. I didn't leave another message. Arantxa, it seemed, was now my ex-girlfriend. I thought about going up to her home, but she would probably refuse to see me. The house would be a mask of indifference. Her family were old money Galicians, old conservative money. They were now pulling up the drawbridge, distancing themselves and their daughter from anything to do with Sofia's disappearance.

I knew of Sofia before I met her. I had already heard her playing the saxophone, the notes painting the air outside her third floor window. When I had asked Arantxa about who the musician was, she had dismissed her. 'Sofia, Sofia Amestoy, she's just a weird, dope-smoking leftie.' It had made me more curious.

A storm had brought heavy rain the morning I first met her. Globs of water exploded on the pavement outside the launderette. She came through the door shaking a small green umbrella. I kept my head in the book I was reading. She was standing over me speaking too rapidly for me to understand. She was pointing to a tattoo on her ankle and saying

'Avispon.' When she realised that I spoke English, she laughed and said, 'Buzzz, buzz,' and pointed to my book. I was reading Stig Larson's *The Girl who Kicked the Hornet's Nest*. She laughed again and offered me her wet hand. 'Hi, I am Sofia,' she said. We chatted about the book and where I was from as she unloaded her clothes from the dryer. Before she left we had exchanged phone numbers.

I tried Arantxa, voicemail again. 'We have to talk,' I said. The air was stifling now, thick with the smell of frying seafood. My shredded coaster was heaped in a neat pile beside the empty wine bottle. I needed to get out, to search for even the whimper of a breeze. I walked down past the Naval Base and out towards the sea. Stronger winds were forecast for tomorrow, but temperatures were to remain high. Perfect wild-fire weather.

The last time I had walked out here was with Sofia. She loved the scent of the pines and the eucalyptus. She said that she could hear the smells and when she played jazz she saw colours in the music. I didn't get that, or jazz really, but I didn't tell her. Later that night we had ended up at the German bar. We could hear the loud voices echoing around the walls before we reached the tiny square. Mathias, the bar owner, was doing most of the shouting. Shouting at Ali, who was goose-stepping up and down while giving Nazi salutes. I was almost laughing, but I could see some of the customers were uneasy and one or two were about to leave. Of course this was angering Mathias even more. Sofia went over to Ali. She lowered his right arm slowly. She joined his two hands and held them between hers, all the while speaking to him very quietly. She took something from her bag and put it between his hands. He backed away slowly, bowing, his hands still joined. Mathias had already turned and walked inside. When I turned my palms upward questioningly she dismissed it all as just different kinds of madness, 'Village blues,' she said. We sat outside and drank wine, Sofia in full flight, music, jazz, and John Coltrane. I listened and watched Mathias wash and dry wine glasses.

The gaps between the peeling eucalyptus trees framed the views out over the estuary. I sat for some time but felt no stillness. It was like listening to bloody John Coltrane. It felt like glass breaking inside my head. That night she had played one of his albums, *A Love Supreme*. For her it was something holy. I found it hard to listen to, it rewired my brain.

A police car drove by, slowly I thought, but maybe I was being paranoid. Anyway it was time to go, another drink in town would soothe the nerves. I took a different route back, up along the stream that ran alongside the allotments, keeping a wary eye out for Ali. I went around to the German bar, hoping it would still be open. Usually Mathias was polite but reserved. Tonight he was more than reserved, almost cold, but I couldn't trust my thoughts anymore.

Like that last night when Ali kicked off. We had drunk a lot. Sofia went inside the bar to use the toilet. I sat outside and looked at the sky, the moon wandering in and out behind the clouds. Then I saw Sofia having a very animated conversation with Mathias, although most conversations in Spain are animated and it's often difficult to tell if it's an argument or not. When she came back out, she picked up the bottle of wine and said, 'Let's go back to my place.'

I watched him now, polishing those precious wine glasses, crystal of course and finely tuned to enhance the aromas and taste. I left and went back to the apartment. Inside the heat was dead and unforgiving. I picked up the L.P. lying on my bed. The cover had a black and white photograph of a very intense looking man and this was his masterpiece, *A Love Supreme*.

Rebecca

Rachel Roberts

She was so utterly infuriated with Stephen, even now, even after all the years that had passed since he left her. Which still struck her as odd, because she hadn't really known him. Not really. Not in the end. So many years she spent pining and missing a man who contributed so much to her life, yet the only residual feeling she could truly identify was her anger. Her absolute rage because he shattered the illusion of her happiness, of her perceived joy, of the life she'd carefully planned and executed for them. Rebecca, in her own insidious way, had moulded a life of expectations Stephen could never meet, and all the while she waited patiently for him to validate her belief that he would one day disappoint her. And in the end he did. She took a disgraceful comfort in knowing she'd been right about him all along, despite the fact that he died.

Stephen had died by suicide. She hated 'committed suicide,' with its archaic religious resonance. Who knows the weight any soul can bear and who gets to judge? There are things in this world too tragic to accept: a toe tag on a toddler where a small sock should be, an old man rotting in a cold bed. The absolute agony of knowing the man you loved took a rope, tied it around his neck, secured it to the ceiling, and jumped.

She would never know the last thoughts that went through his mind. Was it his mother, his first kiss? Was it the way her hair smelled, or the beach he loved? Did he have all these thoughts and still want to jump, or did the torture of leaving all this behind force him to claw at the robe, scratching at his neck, writhing in terror as he realised it was already too late? Or did he simply hang limply and welcome in the death that was the only solution he felt he had left – a solution which only asked more questions than it answered.

His death was a cruel final betrayal, and it had broken her. It made her heart close hard and fast around the idea that she would ever be happy again. The guilt wore her down daily, fuelled her survival, and lent her a purpose. Yet, lurking just beneath her anger was the horrifying fact that maybe she deserved this pain, that her part in his death was perhaps not a small one. His final act, his last autonomous achievement – to bring her as much pain as possible so she could always know, would always remember, just how much she had failed him in their relationship, in their friendship, and in his life. He won the final battle, making sure that this time, at least, he would have the last word. She could argue and rage with a dead man all she liked – but he would always have the last word!

Rebecca was only too aware that the person she'd been in her past was a creation, an aid for making sense of who she'd become in the present. She was a person who believed her happiness was perfect, was real, was a concrete reality she could touch and taste. She looked back now with an ache because she'd missed that happiness – she had missed it – all while it was happening. How, even contained in their arguments, their simmering silences, and in every other simple thing – the love was always there. She resented him for that, for not seeing the truth of their life together, abhorred herself more for holding on to that question she was always – always – too afraid to ask him.

So when Luca entered her life, Rebecca really wasn't paying attention. She had stopped noticing men. Paid less attention when they noticed her. It was just easier that way. But the first time she really observed him was at a dinner party. She sensed someone scrutinising her from the end of the table, drinking her in. When she looked up and met his eyes she was struck at the intensity of a feeling she could barely remember. She felt hot and uncomfortable, but defiant and resilient. She attempted to dismiss the feelings immediately, but she couldn't refute that part of her, lying dormant, had been woken up by his glance, his smile, and the shape his lips made when they formed her name.

She met him again a few weeks later and quietly noted that, despite herself, she liked him. He was curious, interesting, and funny. Younger than she was, Luca was light – free and easy – complicated in the uncomplicated way only the young can be, before life turns hairs grey and bodies soft with worry. She envied that piece of him, wanting desperately to preserve his vulnerability, to protect him from what bitter experience would teach him. To guard him from knowing that life would never be the expectation, limes would never grow from lemon trees, and not all reasons can be accepted as truths we hold and share. She would never be ready to hear the cynicism in his voice as life turned him hard, twisted him into the type of man she could have no reason to love – and she missed having a reason.

Her longing to be around Luca greatly disturbed her, forced her to live with the silent but noxious fear that bearing witness to her brokenness, her neediness, he would one day deny her his affection. Yet, as she slowly, cautiously, and gently unravelled the truth of her fragility, he never did. It simply drew him as close as she was able to let him. He softly offered her permission to feel accepted in her fragments, daring her to consider the honesty of his view. Hesitant to acknowledge her fondness for him, she allowed a tentative friendship to form. Her budding affection unsettled her, an attachment that was terrifying in its familiarity. Their deep conversations challenged her view of the world around her, their laughter and frivolity make her dare to hope. But Luca wasn't Stephen. And Rebecca wasn't sure she was ready to excuse him for that yet, or to forgive Stephen for leaving her either.

Luca invited her to spend Christmas with him and his family in Rome. She was flattered, but unsure. Theirs was a friendship so unsullied she wasn't ready, or prepared, for the possibility of it becoming more. Yet he'd awoken something in her that needed her attention, an awareness of a deep need – to be seen, for passion, for her body to be explored, caressed, and worshipped by new hands, for all the pleasures she had denied herself since Stephen died. In the end, his insistence on wanting to spend the holidays with her wore her down. Although struggling, she accepted his invitation. She agreed to go.

He met her at the airport closest to the city, and when she saw him she was surprised at how happy it made her. This simple gesture of picking her up. How tender he was with his embrace, how carefully he took her bags and carried them to the car, how happy he was to see her. This made her wary. She searched his face for insight, but was met with only his dark, smiling eyes.

When they arrived at his parents' house, she found she was nervous. Not because she was afraid to meet them, but she was suddenly struck with the weight of it all. Meeting Luca's parents, being in Rome – the possibility of a fresh memory that didn't include Stephen. She felt the proverbial gnawing at her insides, subtly persuading her to forget she'd ever had a Stephen. She was tempted to surrender the very idea of him, to return all the moments they'd shared to the time that had existed before they did. She didn't know how to move to a happiness where Stephen, her beautiful Stephen, wouldn't feature.

And he was beautiful, not just physically, which he was, but in a way that made everyone in his sphere feel worthy, at peace with the world, and seen. He was loving, gentle, intelligent, and careful with others' feelings. This man she had built her joy around, whom she had once loved so ferociously, would no longer be a part of her story. Had written himself out. That would always hurt – that he had not loved her enough to stay. It was easier to stay angry with him for that simple truth. He'd sworn his life to her. Now she existed with nothing but tainted memories bouncing around a house hollowed out with pain. He'd left her with nothing but wanting.

Her head was so full with all of this she hadn't notice Luca's mother standing in front of her. Rebecca extended her hand, smiled, and was welcomed into their home.

Luca's childhood home was not how she had imagined it would be, but she observed with delight his absolute pleasure at seeing her there, at watching her drinking coffee and chatting in broken English with his mother. Later that week she asked him to show her 'his Rome,' so he took her to the places in his neighbourhood he'd played as a child, where he'd studied, worked, laughed, and loved. She liked this vignette into his past, enjoyed watching his dark eyes share his secrets. But there was a certain sense of unease about him, as though he couldn't quite understand where it all had gone, couldn't quite find his place anymore. As if time had deceived him, even though he found everything was exactly where and how he left it. It was an intimate moment in his world, and she was aware that in showing her all these parts of his life, he was welcoming her into his story. And in doing so, perhaps starting a new one just for them.

Together they explored the beautiful city. Dark men sold cheap trinkets at every corner, plying tourists with tales of love. They weren't, as she first thought, simply clever marketing ploys, but rather, real stories of their real love. She gave them money not necessarily for the trinkets, nor simply out of pity, but because she recognised their delicate truth, bore witness to their reality. She wanted to cry for them and the struggles their love had brought them. She wanted to cry *at* the beauty, and *for* the beauty of it all. Rome is a city for lovers, a place to be loved. To find it, to seek it, to miss it, and to hope for it.

The day they stood at the top of the *Piazza del Popolo* he asked a passing tourist to take their picture. She turned brightly towards the camera and flinched a little as she felt his warm hand on the small of her back.

He moved his hand around to her waist and pulled her in closer. She fit neatly into his embrace, as if all along it had been waiting for her. She looked up at his strong jaw, at the fine shape of his nose, and sighed heavily. She wanted him to look at her and see everything she couldn't say, yet she couldn't meet his eyes. Like all the other times since Stephen died, she couldn't allow herself to be close to anyone, was too afraid to ask the question that burned her lips. She started to cry then, softly and quietly. Luca turned and looked at her, curious about her tears. She smiled and blamed the sun for her streaming eyes. He put his arm around her and kissed her tenderly on the forehead. He never pressed her for answers, never quizzed her on matters she wasn't ready to share.

At the end of her trip as he drove her to the airport, she stared out the window, afraid her tired, watery eyes would betray her. He was beautiful. There were no other words to describe him. But his beauty brought the pain of all she was afraid to covet.

When they arrived, he carefully took her bags out of the car and walked her to the terminal. They made plans to connect when he was back in the city. She watched him walk away, suddenly so aware of just how much she was going to miss him. And yet in that same moment she wanted to run after him, punch him hard in the face, and beg him to leave her alone because the price of loving him was a cost she could not bear.

His hand was reaching for the exit door when she called him. He turned and walked back towards her. His confident gait made her smile, regardless of her stifled panic. He asked her if everything was okay, a curious smile on his face. She tried to speak, but couldn't. He opened his arms and pulled her into his chest. She could feel his breath at her ear, hear his heartbeat, smell his fresh sweat. He was delicious. He pulled away from the embrace and told her he loved her. His declaration ripe with potential, raw with emotion – his heart open, tender, willing. She looked up into his gorgeous imploring eyes. In order to love him she would have to let go of her anger, her twisted, justified, exhausting anger. The words hung heavy in the space between them. She reached up and placed a hand on his cheek. He waited. Then he sighed, put his own hand over hers, took it from his cheek, and kissed it. Their window closed. But he loved her. It was something. She would always have that.

He leaned over and kissed her on the cheek. She noticed the soft curve of the smile that told her he would be okay, but he wouldn't wait for her. Her heart ached for all that had been stolen, for all she had not fought harder to keep.

She watched Luca walk away before heading towards her departure gate. She might always believe that her life with Stephen would have been spectacular, even though she knew he was never the man he could have been. His life, their life, belonged in the shadows now, stuck in a past that never changes, that time only drags forward. She turned to glimpse Luca one more time, but he was already beyond her vision, had moved into that distant space where she would not follow.

The Turf Cutter

Johnny Thompson

'Come on, where are you taking me . . . this isn't a joke anymore.' The blindfold obscured day from night and put time out of kilter. He was unable to discern how long he had been there or who he was with or indeed where he had come from. All he knew was that he was now walking, outside. The smell of trees and earth hung in the air, his other senses heightened by this enforced lack of vision. He tried to reason again, but was met with silence, a dread-filled void, save the sound of footsteps. His own and maybe just one other, or perhaps there was someone with a lighter step in the background? He pleaded again, worried that this was now a deadly serious situation. 'Look, let's talk, there's nothing we can't work out, please talk to me, man. Is it about money? Seriously, if it is, then no worries, we can sort something, I can give you whatever you want.' No response.

The feeling he was experiencing was alien to him. He did not recognise fear because it rarely visited him, had not for years anyway. Now this brutal raw emotion felt like a skeletal claw scraping his gut and another rapping mercilessly inside his skull, his burning fear growing towards terror. He tried to reason again but the words were stuck fast in his throat. An angry response would have been welcome, something to negotiate with, but no sound, except for the footsteps.

The disembodied talon was now beating an angry staccato in his head, pounding and forcing salty tears through the blindfold and on to his face. He tasted the tears and felt a new sensation blending with the other fertile emotions. The tears brought shame, a feeling of weakness and cowardice that he would never have allowed anyone else to see. Now whoever was holding him could witness his shame, making him feel very small and vulnerable at that moment. The silence continued, pregnant with possibilities he could not contemplate. A heavy uncharted emptiness. Then nothing.

Tom opened his eyes and blinked a couple of times. The sheer whiteness of the walls and curtains in St Mary's Ward was always an assault, particularly so in the middle of the day, with the sun hopping off every surface. He attempted to sit up gingerly in the bed, aware of the endless tubes and wires that snaked around his arms and abdomen as he slowly negotiated a new position. No pain thankfully. The pump was doing its job in that respect.

The ward was quiet. No doctors swarming around, and visiting time had not yet commenced. There were a couple of nurses at the medication trolley, and the calm was enhanced by Billy, the care assistant, being on his lunch break. Billy Kavanagh, the man who could converse with himself, asking questions and answering them before a second voice could be heard. Tom liked him, but also liked the monumental silence during Billy's absence.

Tom had been offered a move to the side room, an hour after the team had mentioned words like terminal and palliative. The nurse mentioned a hospice bed, though this would have meant his small number of visitors having to travel, and he didn't want to inconvenience anyone else. Declining the side room was easy as he didn't think he'd want to be staring at four white walls waiting to check out. Instead he opted to stay in main ward. There was comfort in noise and activity, serenity in company, and Tom was content to be where he was. He'd done the anger and bargaining stages and was now resigned to his fate. He knew this was the departure lounge, non-refundable and no return journey.

Tom was struggling to sit up when Billy arrived back from his lunch. Billy was commentating in a dramatic radio voice on a historic match as he weaved down the ward, hurling an imaginary sliotar as he moved. 'Tom Duff has the ball for the Saints, he moves majestically past two defenders and dissects the posts with a magnificent point! The Saints have taken the lead!' His voice trailed off as he saw that Tom was having difficulty and rushed to help him sit up.

'Here you go, Tom. God, I remember that day well, I was a small boy watching you from the stand with my father. 1979, the Saints winning the county senior, what age were you then Tom? Twenty-three, I reckon?'

That was Billy, answering his own question without a momentary pause. He was still talking as he moved Tom into a sitting position.

'Who is coming in today, Tom? Brigid maybe, or Old Jessup? Anyway let's get you sorted for the visit and see who arrives.'

Billy left, still reminiscing about Tom's prowess on the hurling field. At this stage he was telling a disinterested student nurse that Tom had only ever been sent off once in a career spanning thirty years.

'Your man Cassidy, a dirty animal, gave young Donovan from the Saints an awful skelp of a hurl, nearly took the head clean work off his shoulders. Well that was the rock he perished on. Tom Duff had to be dug out of Cassidy. He gave him a few unmerciful wallops, all deserved to be fair. No red cards in them days, just off with ye and no talking back.'

Tom purposely zoned out. He had heard the story relayed time and time again. He wasn't proud of that particular incident, but he was blessed, or maybe cursed with a protective nature and would never deny that. Little Mark Donovan had done nothing to deserve the bullying Cassidy was meting out on the pitch. Tom fixed that. He closed his eyes and dozed peacefully.

❧❧❧

Brigid had arrived and was sitting on the edge of the bed by the time he woke, smiling, though her eyes were filled with a resigned melancholy. Tom was eager to take the conversation away from illness, so threw her off guard with his opening gambit.

'Nice day for the bog isn't it? The old lady would have been up and ready at seven bells with a roll of Goulding's bags under her oxter.'

Brigid laughed at the memory, the four of them in the Morris Minor heading to cut and heap turf for the day. Or, as the summer progressed, filling empty fertiliser bags in readiness to draw the turf home.

Tom was regarded as an artist with the slean, his mother boasting that her boy could slice a Christmas pudding with the turfman's tool. Their father was long since passed, leaving Gertie Duff with three children to rear. Tom was the eldest, hence the acclaimed turf cutters role, then Paul and then Brigid the baby, with only a few short years separating the three. Mammy had worked hard to raise the family, cleaning and washing in Old Jessup's house until Tom left school and went to work for him as well.

'Hard to believe she is ten years gone.' Brigid broke the momentary silence. 'God, Tom she worked hard, all her bloody life. But Paul broke her heart, she was never the same after.' Her voice was uneven, eyes misty as she fought back the memories.

Paul had always been Gertie's prime concern. His wild antics and lust for the highlife kept her awake for countless nights, just waiting for him to roll home. Paul had an untimely demise, knocked down by a speeding car after a cocktail of drink and drugs had rendered him incapable of walking home safely. He was in the company of a group of lads Tom's age, lads that Tom had grown up with, and that Tom now mainly avoided.

Sergeant Connolly had informed them after the funeral that a 'few scobies' had been questioned about the availability of drugs and names of suppliers but had met a wall of silence. Though the world and its mother, and indeed Paul Duff's mother, knew who was peddling drugs in the town in the 80s, there was never enough evidence to convict anyone. Tom had spoken to Connolly before, out of a sense of worry that Paul was going in the wrong direction. He couldn't really say with any certainty that Paul's 'friends' were dealing drugs, but he knew it wasn't beyond possibility.

Brigid changed the subject. 'Was Liz in to see you?'

'Nah, not yet. She would want to come sometime soon though.'

Brigid smiled at this. Even in the darkest times Tom would draw a smile from her. She liked Liz Jackson and had always imagined Tom being happy with her. But insofar as she could ever guess, Tom's love for Liz was unrequited. 'Mammy wasn't too keen on Liz, was she, Tom?'

'Nope, she was not. Remember when she saw Liz at Mass in the mini skirt?'

Brigid finished the story, mimicking Gertie Duff's stern voice, 'Not enough cloth in it to tighten the head of a spade.' Now they both laughed, as they had when they were kids chasing Paul across the bog whilst Mammy was getting the sandwiches and red lemonade sorted for the lunch.

Brigid had left the three of them in the house after falling in love with Tony, a Tullamore lad who had asked her to dance when Tweed were belting out "Bohemian Rhapsody" in the Harriers club. Now they were busy managing a pub in Kings Langley and looking after three kids. She 'came home' every summer for the cemetery Mass, and for a week at Christmas. Tom looked forward to the madness of three kids running wild around the house, knowing Mammy loved that time as well.

After Paul's death and Brigid's moving to England, it was just him and Mammy in the house. Second Mass every Sunday, unless he was hurling or making a rare appearance for the soccer club. On those occasions it was Saturday evening Mass and an ice cream in Delaney's on the way home. Mammy preferred Sunday morning, and the visit to Paul and Daddy with a few flowers before heading home for the roast. Comfort and familiarity, all gone when she succumbed to the same callous invasion he was now experiencing in his body. Since then Tom lived alone, relishing the visits by the half Offaly crew more than they would understand.

The days can roll together when you are lying in bed waiting for the tall man with the cloak and scythe to turn up. Tom was unsure if Brigid had gone back to England, or if she was at home in the cottage cleaning around busily like Mammy had done for all her life. He was listening to Billy rabbiting on, pretending to be asleep through awkward embarrassment. 'See him beside you there, Joe? That's Tom Duff, legendary stick man with the Saints and should have got more runs with the County only for their stupid politics.'

Poor old Joe shifted uncomfortably in his bed, feigning interest in Billy's tales about Tom. 'Thing is, right, he could have and should have a Whitley Cup medal with the soccer lads as well. They beat Killavilla in the semi-final. Tom there scored two and the stupid ref ruined the day by disallowing a perfectly good third goal. Anyway, they won two nil, and Tom couldn't play the final, he was hurling the same day. The lads won and poor Tom never got a sniff of a medal.'

Tom had to wake now, open his eyes, as he sensed that someone was sitting by his bed. The soft smell of pipe tobacco and the dry cough told him it was Mr Jessup, or Old Jessup as he was known. 'Well, Thomas.'

'Hello, Mr Jessup, good of you to come.'

Jessup leaned forward in the chair, smiling beneath his coiffured moustache, 'Thomas, I think you could chance calling me Elliot at this stage.'

Elliot Jessup was of an indeterminable age. He had a shock of grey hair, combed back and tied in a ponytail and the most elegant moustache imaginable. He was not typical of his years, or indeed his station in life, undertaker and part-time farmer on a small holding just outside the town. He lived alone and had company maybe once a year when his brother Claude would visit from Dublin.

Claude owned a funeral parlour in the city centre, located in his late father's coffin joinery workshop. The brothers learnt their trade from Gregor and listened intently to his stories of fleeing Poland when his family were hunted down like animals by Nazi troops. They were both born in the safety of Dublin but were both proud and conscious of the bravery of their family in the face of terror. Gregor instilled honesty, loyalty, and manners into his boys, traits they carried into their wintering years.

Elliot first saw Thomas Duff while walking his dogs across the bog on a sweltering summer's day. He stopped to light a pipe and noted that Gertrude, or Miss Duff as he called her, was working feverishly with her three children. Well, two children. The blonde middle son had run off, incurring the wrath of his mother from a safe distance. He watched intently as the eldest boy cut the turf, each sod a replica of the last, and fired them from the slean above his head for his mother and sister to lay on the crusted surface. He immediately liked the cut of this boy and quietly asked Gertrude if Tom would be interested in some work. Tom was never keen on school, and when he turned sixteen he went to work for Mr Jessup, initially on the farm and eventually in the funeral home, and then digging graves with the same uncanny symmetry he showed cutting sods of wet turf.

Tom was about to speak when the solace was interrupted by Billy. 'Well, Tom, you are back with us! Good man. Mr Jessup is here to visit.' That was it. Off Billy sauntered after his gem of stating the obvious.

Tom had begun planning with Elliot for his final journey. Burial with the family, with a few sandwiches and soup in Hennessy's after the graveyard. 'Obviously, everything goes to Brigid, the house and car, and a few bob in the bank, I sorted that with Mortimer. And there is a good few quid, an envelope behind the siding of the bath, some of it to cover your bill. I am not telling her about it because she'll panic, maybe you would let her know when . . . '

He stopped, and Elliot Jessup grabbed his arm in a reassuring touch. 'Leave it with me, Thomas, say no more.'

He wouldn't be taking money from Brigid for this work, but he couldn't tell Tom that. Pride would have caused an argument, and Elliot held Tom in too high regard to have an unseemly squabble at this stage of their long relationship. Instead he smiled and held Tom's hand for a moment.

'Thank you, my dearest friend, for your loyalty and your friendship over the years. We both know the journey is almost complete. It has been my incredible honour to have known you.' Tears were trickling down Elliot's chiselled cheekbone as he spoke, but he made no manful attempt to stem the flow. His words were honest, from the heart, and Tom appreciated the moment. He was more than just an employer, he was a friend, a man to whom Tom had turned for advice and assistance on many occasions.

'No sir, *thank you!* You got me out of a few scrapes and you always had faith in me. Remember, plant me on the left, over Paul. Mammy was planted in on top of Father's side.'

To the uneducated ear the request might sound crass and ugly, but between two men who carried out such requests with a sense of grace and dignity there was a modicum of the ordinary in the conversation.

Tom felt considerably weaker. He was unable to rise in the bed, and any movements required Billy to assist. He reckoned the best barometer of how the illness had progressed was the reduction in chat by Billy Kavanagh. It was as if a respect filter was automatically switched on in Billy's head. The epitome of professionalism. As he lifted Tom in the bed and shook out the pillows behind him, he spoke quietly. 'Good man, Duff, you are a trooper, a hero to me anyway.' Tom knew it was meant. Some things in life were, and some simply were not.

As expected Liz visited late one sultry afternoon, so warm and humid it reminded Tom of wild thunderstorms on the bog, with Mammy shouting at them to get into the Minor and Paul playfully hiding and driving her mad.

'Hello, Tom.'

He looked up. Liz Jackson, or Leggy Lizzie as she was called in school, was tall and elegant and in a different world would have been turning heads at fashion shows in Milan or Paris. Tom was besotted by her when they were growing up, but never had the courage to tell her, or to even send an unsigned Valentine's card in case she knew it was him. He answered her now, albeit feebly, and she motioned to him to rest easy.

'Don't talk, Tom, I can do that for both of us.'

He gazed at her without any words for a few moments. She was sixty years old with a sense of wisdom and sadness in her eyes. Her life had been difficult, a drunk father who mistreated his family and left them penniless and splintered when he had a massive heart attack. In the pub, with a half-finished large bottle on the counter. Then a difficult marriage that left her further broken and facing an arduous uphill battle to get control of her life. She seemed content now, and despite that mournful sadness that haunted you when you looked deep into her eyes, she was at least able to smile.

Tom remembered his first plan to ask her out, 1979, and a dinner dance in honour of the Saints county champions team. He had a new suit, courtesy of Elliot Jessup, and a few pounds in his pocket. All he needed was to ask.

Old Jessup had cajoled him. 'Make your move, Thomas. She will not be free forever.'

He made up his mind to ask her to dance when they went to the Indians in Borris, one Friday night a few weeks prior to the dance. He had the usual Friday evening. Cycle home from the farm, haircut and blow dry with Delia in Clever Cuts and then a few pints in Hennessy's. Then run for the bus to Borris and watch Big Chief and the Indians whooping up a storm in the Ossory Club. He had another pint there and plucked up the courage to ask her to dance, but despite several rounds of the hall, Liz Jackson was nowhere to be seen. She must have shifted someone else.

Tom felt a gnawing emptiness in his stomach, wanting to go home but resigned to waiting for the bus. Big Chief was now doing a feverish war dance across the stage, howling at an imaginary moon, greasepaint luminous in the strobe lighting. It felt surreal and cloying, and Tom made his way outside to get some air. Unfortunately Liz was engaged in a kiss with Mick Muldoon beside the bus when he went out, an incongruous sight, her six feet tall and bent over whilst Mick at five foot nothing was on his tippy toes returning the kiss. Tom was gutted. He hated Mick 'the Lip' with a vengeance.

The Lip had received his nickname when he wore a new leather jacket to school and told Miss Murphy that he looked a bit like Mick Jagger. The jacket was combined with faded denim jeans held up by a leather belt and an impossibly big metal buckle with the Southern Cross emblazoned on it. It was the Lip's new trademark, even though he was totally clueless about the origins and meaning or significance of the image on the buckle. He liked the nickname though, as it gave him a sense of wellbeing. He was a leader, despite his lack of physical stature, and had a crew of hard chaws hanging with him on all occasions. It was to Tom's eternal dismay that Paul had latched on to this crew, had become part of the gang in his own mind, even if they didn't fully accept him. Gertie Duff had warned Paul about getting involved with 'That Muldoon thug, he isn't the size of a Jack Russell with his big dogs all around him. Little good-for-nothing consequence.' Paul had laughed her warning off, and it was both Tom's and Gertie's earnest belief that the Lip was with Paul the night he died. Nothing was ever proven though.

As time moved on Liz fell deeper and deeper in love with Mick the Lip, and eventually married him with a massive wedding in the Montague, partially or wholly funded by the Lip's alleged nefarious dealings in illicit substances. The fairy-tale romance didn't last long though. Sightings of Leggy Lizzie became few and far between, and when she was out in public, she was often wearing sunglasses and long-sleeved shirts, a long way from the movie star bride the Lip had married. Tom despaired for her, cursed the moment she took up with that toerag and hated himself for not asking her out sooner. Now looking at her from his death-bed he knew he was still in love with her, and that the chances were she always knew it.

His mind wandered back a few years to a Saturday night in Hennessy's when he was having a pint after a Saints match. Mick the Lip and crew were in the pub, noisy and boisterous and intimidating the older regulars who were in for a quiet drink and maybe a game of Twenty-fives. The Lip and his main sidekick, a hulk called Cav McEvoy, were in particularly raucous humour, flicking beer at passersby and behaving like kids. Liz was sitting meekly between them, pretending not to notice and yet smiling nervously when the Lip looked at her for approval for another moment of silliness.

McEvoy had received his nickname from a teacher in the Community school called Ned Dillon, during a particularly disruptive mechanical drawing class. 'McEvoy, with the big thick nut on you, your outsized head looks like a cavity block: big, thick, square, and really very empty.' Now he was simply Cav, a shortened derivative of Cavity Block.

The Lip spotted Tom and shouted to him, 'Hey, hero, come and have a pint with me and the missus.'

Tom declined, made an excuse and went towards the bar, but Muldoon was not satisfied. He turned to Liz and sneered, 'Hey Lizzie, do you see Tom there? Remember when he was after you like a sick puppy? Then you met a real man, isn't that right, babe?'

Tom tried not to react, kept looking behind the bar and away from the table where the trio were seated. 'He wanted to do a line with you!' The Lip was building pace now with the teasing. 'But sure his retard brother liked an ould line as well, isn't that right, Cav?'

McEvoy snorted out laughter, finished a pint, and stood up to go to the bar. Tom moved, he set towards the Lip, aware that McEvoy would move behind him. Years of hurling in tight corners taught you how to manoeuvre, and Tom knew he would have a bottle from the bar to clock McEvoy and still rain a few blows on the Lip. Muldoon showed no fear though, and that unnerved Tom a bit.

'Now now, Duff man, go easy,' teased the Lip. 'There's more than you and me in this dance.'

At first Tom thought that big Cav McEvoy was the third wheel in the waltz, but a quick glance into Lizzie's eyes told him different. He knew from the misery in her eyes that whatever retribution he took on her husband now would be revisited on her tenfold when the Lip got her alone. Tom walked away, tensed with anger and listening to one last jibe.

'Go home to your ould Mammy Duff, only woman you'll see tonight.'

As he was leaving the pub Sergeant Ger Connolly spoke to him at the door. 'Well done, Tom.' That was all that needed saying.

Shortly after that Mick the Lip up and left town, without as much as a goodbye to his wife. All of his ill-gotten monies were missing, though the Guards found some drugs and a handgun under the floorboards in his bathroom. Rumours were abound surrounding his disappearance. One scenario had him running away with an Albanian crime lord's daughter, another had him executed in a field by dissident republicans who were tired of his shenanigans in their area of expertise. Someone else reported seeing him and Cav McEvoy with a known Dublin criminal in a hotel in Dubai, with a bevy of beautiful women surrounding them. McEvoy was questioned by the Guards around the time the Lip had gone, but despite robust questioning Cav would not yield any information on his boss. The only certainty was that Mick the Lip had left Dodge and few were bothered looking for him.

Whatever the reason, the gift of time and his absence made Lizzie return to her former cheerful self. She eventually started venturing out and occasionally met Tom for a coffee in town, chatting about the old days but never mentioning Mick Muldoon, or any part of her life with him. Now as the light was dwindling on Tom's life, she felt an enormous sense of love for the man. She never loved Tom Duff in the way that star-crossed lovers do, but she loved the reliability and the reassurance of him. She leaned over the bed and kissed Tom gently on the lips. For that moment of silence, Tom felt a sense of total peace and calm. Then, nothing.

Ger Connolly was in his slippers, doing the Times crossword when the young officer rapped his door. Connolly donned a pair of hiking boots and an anorak and followed the Guard to the squad car, hopping in as the blue light was switched on and the engine gunned. When they arrived at the location he was greeted by a young detective.

'Sergeant Connolly, thanks for coming. My name is Michael Maloney. I am the senior here tonight. I thought we might need your help, as this was your old stomping ground before you retired.'

It was more of a statement than a question, and Connolly left it unanswered. The night sky was lit by lamps on tripods surrounding a large white tent, and figures in white overalls and masks were taking photographs and various samples as they neared the entrance to the tent. Maloney handed him a paper mask, which Connolly fixed over his mouth and nose. He had never been here after dark and was uncomfortable being here now. The smell of earth and pine trees hung in the air.

Inside the tent the ground had been opened in a uniformly rectangular shape. Maloney explained, 'Couple of lads working today, opened here instead of there, and then we were alerted. I thought you would want a look before the tech boys tear it asunder.'

Ger Connolly peered over the edge of the hole, an arc lamp pointed downwards illuminated the scene. The decomposed body of a man lay across a wooden box, approximately four feet below ground level. Connolly surveyed the body, the still shiny belt buckle resting across the wasted midriff. A large Southern Cross glinting in the light.

'So, Mick the Lip, that's where you disappeared to.'

He looked at the partially concealed cross at the head of the grave. He could just make out 'Gertrude Duff, Rest in Peace.'

Connolly smiled to himself and whispered gently, 'Well done, Tom.'

What Goes Around

Katy White

It was a clear March morning when Simon's wife told him that she was leaving him for another man. The day began as usual – Kara berated him for leaving a wet towel on the bed, Simon looked vaguely surprised even though this happened every morning, Kara tripped over his shoes in the hall and gave out to him for leaving them there, Kara picked up the jam pot by the lid and it promptly fell to the floor, which prompted her to complain that he never screwed the lids on jars properly.

'I'm sorry,' said Simon, 'but maybe you should stop picking jars up by the lids then.'

Kara looked at him, the jam lid still in one hand, raspberry jam splattered like blood at her feet. 'I'm leaving you.'

Simon paused with a forkful of poached egg halfway to his mouth. 'Over a jar of jam?'

'No!' Kara exclaimed. 'I've met someone else. I'm in love with him. And you're getting egg all over your tie.' She flung a tea towel at him, and he looked down in surprise at the bright yellow blooming on his chest.

'Who is he, then? How did you meet him?'

'He works at Fenwick's,' she said, referencing the local grocer.

'I see.' Simon did not recall any of the staff at Fenwick's being particularly handsome or charming. Or even good at their job. This comforted him, and he stood up from the table, leaving his poached eggs half-eaten.

'I'll be gone when you get home from work,' said Kara. Simon looked at her in her too-short pyjamas, with the raspberry jam splotched around her bare feet, and felt his heart cringe, as if he had just witnessed someone kick a small animal. He took his coat from the back of the chair and left the house without saying anything.

Forty minutes later, Simon was pulling into his assigned parking space (three from the top) outside the office where he worked. It was a large, inoffensive brown building in a busy part of the city, set back slightly from the surrounding offices just far enough so that you couldn't see the company name from the street. When people asked Simon what he did for a living, he told them that he did the accounts for a large firm, which was, in a sense, true. This sounded boring enough that no one ever questioned him further, and indeed the office exterior looked boring enough that no passer-by ever remarked upon it, let alone considered that a substantial amount of the opportunities and challenges they faced in their lifetime was determined within its four walls.

The 'M' in the company logo behind the reception desk was dangling by a thread and made Simon clench his jaw as he walked by it, which he told himself was because he had emailed maintenance about fixing it two weeks ago. He was still thinking about the 'M' when he got to his office on the third floor, so he flicked on his computer and started to write a strongly worded email to the maintenance department. His brain suddenly conjured an image of Kara packing all of her clothes into a suitcase and taking her toothbrush from their shared en-suite, which interrupted his concentration and made his chest feel heavy and tight.

A knock on the door forced his attention onto the present. The slow, controlled exhale he had been using to calm the frightening feeling in his chest became a sigh when his intern, Kevin, popped his head around the door.

'Morning, boss,' he chirped. 'I brought you a coffee, and I also have a few questions about some of the cases we were discussing yesterday. You know the lady who ran the marathon to raise money for cancer, and we were going to look into her winning a holiday on the radio? Well I was just thinking, it actually turns out that her husband has cancer, just recently diagnosed actually, so I was wondering if we could cure that? And also . . .'

The heaviness in Simon's chest radiated up his neck and into his head, settling as a dull ache behind his eyes. He was aware that Kevin was still talking, but the enthusiasm and curiosity in his voice seemed like such alien concepts to Simon that he might as well have been speaking a different language. There was another knock at the door, and the bespectacled, perpetually concerned face of his colleague Anita appeared behind Kevin. Simon didn't like Anita – she was always unloading difficult cases on him – but he welcomed her interruption at that moment.

'Kevin, leave my coffee on the desk,' he said, beckoning Anita into the room. 'Yes, what is it?'

'I have a few difficult cases I'm unsure of,' she began, and Simon felt the ache behind his eyes intensify. He gestured at her to continue. Kevin hovered beside his desk.

'Well, first off, this man stole an old lady's grocery shopping when she was coming out of the supermarket. However, it was to feed his family as he recently lost his job, so I'm not sure if that warrants—'

'Have his car break down, with all the tyres needing to be replaced,' Simon said swiftly, taking a sip of his coffee. 'Next.' Anita began scribbling rapidly on the file in her hands.

'Okay, this next case about the woman adopting the three abandoned dogs she found – we instructed for her to win a holiday on the radio, but that got rejected because we've reached our holiday quota for the month so—'

'That will fit perfectly with what I was saying!' Kevin interjected, 'We can swap out my case, cure her husband's cancer and give this other woman the holiday on the radio.' Anita nodded and continued scribbling. 'Okay, great, so then if we could just—'

'No!' Simon slammed his palm down on the desk, which wasn't something he had ever done before, and he was surprised by how much it hurt. 'No,' he repeated in a friendlier voice, trying to inject some lightness into his tone as Anita and Kevin both looked alarmed. 'The marathon runner, she doesn't meet the criteria for miracle cure; we can't just hand those things out like sweets. Give the dog lady some kind of lottery winning instead.'

Anita wrote this down carefully. 'Okay, and then we just have this case of this married woman who has an ongoing affair with an employee at the local grocer. I'm not sure of the protocol if the affair has been going on for longer than six months?'

At the word 'grocer,' Simon felt very hot and then very cold. He was aware that Anita and Kevin were looking at him expectantly, and also suddenly very aware of the egg stain on his tie. 'Leave that file with me,' he said hoarsely. Anita frowned.

'I have to submit it by 5 pm or else it's not going to—'

'Leave it with me,' Simon repeated tersely. 'Now please leave, both of you, I have an important phone call to make.' Anita left the file on his desk, and she and Kevin both walked out of the room.

Simon looked at the file perched innocently on his desk. He didn't even have to open it. He knew what it contained. He should report it – that's what the standard procedure was in this scenario. It happened from time to time: a case trickled through that had personal relevance to whomever was managing it, and you had to report it because you couldn't objectively manage a personal case. He was going to have to fill out a report form, and declare that the woman in this file was his wife, and that she had been cheating on him for more than six months with an employee from the grocer's, and then he would submit the report to the head office, and they would redistribute the case. A thought occurred to him: he wasn't managing the case – Anita was. She just happened to ask for his guidance on it. He knew what the protocol for an affair lasting more than six months was – a level 5 sanction – so that is what he should authorise in this case. He glanced at the half-completed email on his computer screen, littered with obscenities. The 'M' in the company logo stood for 'moral,' but Simon felt it would be more fitting if it stood for 'marriage' since that was what most of their cases seemed to revolve around, in one way or another. He pressed the delete button on the email. With the 'M' falling off, the company name read 'K. A. R. ~. A.' in big letters, which gave him a big headache when he thought about it. 'Knowledgeable Authority Regarding Moral Affairs.' Simon didn't feel very knowledgeable about anything at the moment.

He reflected on the possible reasons why Kara could be leaving him. She said she was in love with someone else, this guy from the grocer's. It occurred to Simon that this could be a repercussion for something he himself had done. But a spouse having an affair was a level 6 sanction, and he couldn't think of anything that he had done that would warrant that. Kara must be leaving him because she wanted to leave him, not because the authority had arranged it. It was true that she was often angry at him and told him frequently how fed up she was of him. There was an endless list of things he did that infuriated her. He wondered how he should handle this case – what should he advise Anita? How many people got to decide the consequences faced by their spouse for having an affair? He imagined imposing any of the level 5 sanctions – losing your job, having your house burgled, developing an allergy to your favourite food – on Kara, and felt like laughing and crying simultaneously. He scribbled a list of suggestions on a green sticky note and stuck it to the front of the file, and then went to find Anita.

Kevin and Anita were both in her office working on a case, which annoyed Simon as soon as he walked in because Kevin was his intern, not Anita's. He handed Anita the file and gave Kevin some vague orders, watching Anita's brow become even more furrowed than usual as she squinted at the green sticky note. 'This seems a bit . . . unconventional?' she queried, looking at him through her ridiculously big glasses.

'It's warranted, given the circumstances,' Simon replied shortly. He made to leave the room.

'Have her trip over her new lover's shoes in the hall?' Anita said, her voice full of concern. 'Have her new lover be unable to close jars properly? Leave wet towels on the bed? Is this in the guidelines?'

'If there's any issue, tell them I authorised it,' Simon said, 'Kevin, I thought I told you to get me another coffee?'

About the Authors

Siobhan Flynn

Siobhan lives in Clonroche, Co. Wexford. She is married, with two grown-up daughters, and an energetic terrier. Siobhan has been writing, sporadically, since childhood. She began writing poetry as a member of a Community Writing group in Wexford in the 1990s, and has had a number of poems published locally, later moving on to the short story format.

Siobhan's stories have been published in *The New Ross Standard, The Leitrim Guardian,* and *Woman's Way* magazine. Two of her stories were shortlisted in *Ireland's Own Anthology of Winning Irish Short Stories* in 2017 and 2018. In 2020 her work appeared in *The Ray D'Arcy Show Anthology,* 'A Page from my Life.' Siobhan says, 'I would love to publish my own collection of short stories, and haven't completely ruled out the possibility of a novel – though this may be on the long finger.'

John Geoghegan

Originally from Galway, but well embedded in Kildare, John has been living in Naas since 1986. 'I was a teacher in Dublin for thirty-four years. I am a member of a writing group, Naas Moat Writers, and have had stories published locally and nationally. Along with other members of our group I have had poems read on Kfm Radio on a number of occasions. I have no favourite genre, I enjoy writing short stories, poetry, and memoir.'

Jillian Godsil

Jillian is an award winning journalist, broadcaster, and author. She loves writing but finds her day job gobbles up her word count allowance at a dangerous pace. Sometimes she worries that she will not have any words left over at the end of the day. 'When God made words, there were zillions of them but maybe not the corresponding and required amount of time.' When not considering matters of such importance, Jillian is a mother to two wonderful young women who teach her daily that learning is less an option than an imperative. Long live the day.

Mary Hanrahan

Mary lives in Tipperary and a lifelong love of words brought her to writing.

A child of the fifties, a convent girl in the swinging sixties, a returned emigrant in the seventies, married in the eighties, teaching in the nineties, learning in the Millenium, writing always. Mary writes short stories, poetry, and radio drama, and has been lucky enough to collaborate with other artists in a number of multi-disciplinary projects.

Laura-Blaise McDowell

Laura-Blaise holds an MA in Creative Writing from UCD. Her fiction and poetry have appeared in publications including *The Irish Times, HeadStuff, Sonder, The Honest Ulsterman,* and *Still Worlds Turning,* an anthology of new Irish writing from No Alibis Press.

She had two short stories on the 2019 Writing.ie Short Story of the Year Award longlist, with *Balloon Animals* making the shortlist. Her short memoir appears in *The Fish Anthology 2020* as part of the Fish Short Memoir Prize. In 2021, her story *The Lobster Waltz* was shortlisted for the Costa Short Story Award.

Helen O'Leary

Helen lives in Nass, County Kildare, and has been writing since her retirement. Twice winner of the June Fest Short Story Competition (2017 and 2020), her work has also been awarded first prizes in The Michael Mullan Writing Competitions (2018, 2019). In 2019 Helen published her first novel, *The Heart Stone*. Helen is a member of the Moat Writers, Nass.

Patrick Orwill

Patrick says he came to the craft of writing late. 'I've always loved words and during the last few years I've surprised myself by how much I enjoy the process of putting words together. This is the first time I have submitted a piece for a literary competition.'

Rachel Roberts

Rachel is an enigmatic soul whose love of creativity evolved from a deeply intuitive hunger for stories which tell us who we are and what we are truly capable of. Her motivation to write is driven by her instinctual need to extract the subtle, yet often unseen truths from those same stories.

Awarded a master's degree in philosophy, in conjunction with a long vocation as a practicing yogi, her writing speaks of the fragility of humanity, and the weight every soul must bear. The truths she sifts through compel her to express that which eludes her; embodying the hallowed stories that her heart is aching to share.

Johnny Thompson

Johnny is a semi-retired mental health nurse and part-time family celebrant. 'I am originally from Mountrath and have lived in Dublin for many years. I am married to Helen and have three adult children. I had dabbled in writing for ages, from satirical sketches to abandoned poetry to unfinished short stories, until Helen gave me the ultimate Christmas present, enrollment in a writing course. Since then I have a bit more purpose to my writing, culminating in being published in this anthology. I am lucky to have some friends to critique my writing, including a select group called Scribes who became firm friends and writing buddies since meeting at the course. In the last while, I have varied from poetry, to short stories, to romantic pieces for my celebrancy engagements.'

Katy White

Katy is currently a student in her twenties with a writing career spanning decades, beginning with a diary she kept for her eight-year-old self's musings. She was first inspired to write by teachers who praised her penmanship for being so neat despite being left-handed – but continued to write because she fell in love with it. She currently writes in a range of formats, from prose to grocery lists, and most recently a blog. She doesn't have much figured out yet, but that which she does can be attributed to writing.

.

www.ingramcontent.com/pod-product-compliance
Lightning Source LLC
Chambersburg PA
CBHW072012170626
46813CB00005B/2129